PUSHKIN
VERTIGO

MARGARET MILLAR (1915–1994) was the author of 27 books and a masterful pioneer of psychological mysteries and thrillers. Born in Kitchener, Ontario, she spent most of her life in Santa Barbara, California, with her husband Ken Millar, who is better known by his nom de plume of Ross Macdonald. Her 1956 novel *Beast in View* won the Edgar Allan Poe Award for Best Novel. In 1965 Millar was the recipient of the *Los Angeles Times* Woman of the Year Award and in 1983 the Mystery Writers of America gave her the Grand Master Award for Lifetime Achievement. Millar's cutting wit and superb plotting have left her an enduring legacy as one of the most important crime writers of both her own and subsequent generations.

"She has few peers, and no superior in the art of bamboozlement"

JULIAN SYMONS, *THE COLOUR OF MURDER*

"Mrs Millar doesn't attract fans, she creates addicts"

DILYS WINN

"She writes minor classics"

VASHINGTON POST

"Very original"

GATHA CHRISTIE

"Margaret Millar was one of th̶e̶ ̶.̶.̶.̶ ̶ ̶s̶u̶s̶p̶e̶n̶s̶e̶, a standout chronicler of inner psychology and the human mind. *Vanish in an Instant* is a perfect gateway to her fiction, after which you'll devour so many more of her classic novels"

SARAH WEINMAN, AUTHOR OF *THE REAL LOLITA* AND EDITOR OF
WOMEN CRIME WRITERS: EIGHT SUSPENSE NOVELS OF THE 1940S & 50S

"The real queen of suspense... Millar's psychologically complex, disturbingly dark thrillers always manage to surprise the reader... She can't write a dull sentence, and her endings always deliver a shock"

CHRISTOPHER FOWLER, AUTHOR OF *THE BRYANT & MAY MYSTERIES*

Vanish in
an Instant

PUSHKIN VERTIGO

MARGARET
MILLAR

Pushkin Press
71–75 Shelton Street
London WC2H 9JQ

Vanish in an Instant was first published by Dell in New York, 1952
First published by Pushkin Press in 2018

1 3 5 7 9 8 6 4 2

ISBN 13: 978-1-78227-479-7

Designed and typeset by Tetragon, London
Printed and bound by CPI Group (UK) Ltd, Croydon CRO 4YY

www.pushkinpress.com

For my loved ones
MILL AND LINDA

ONE

Snow and soot sprinkled the concrete runways like salt and pepper. Twenty miles to the east Detroit was a city of smoke and lights. Twenty miles to the west the town of Arbana was not visible at all, but it was to the west that Mrs. Hamilton looked first as if she hoped to catch a miraculous glimpse of it.

On the observation ramp above the airfield she could see the faces of people waiting to board a plane or to meet someone or simply waiting and watching, because if they couldn't go anywhere themselves, the next best thing was to watch someone else going. Under the glaring lights their faces appeared as similar as the rows of wax vegetables in the windows of the markets back home. She scanned the faces briefly, wondering if one of them belonged to her son-in-law, Paul. She wasn't sure she would recognize him—in her mind he had never entirely taken shape as a person, he was just Virginia's husband—or that he would recognize her.

"*I* certainly haven't changed," she said aloud, quite sharply.

Her companion turned with an air of surprise. She was a slim girl in her early twenties, rather pretty, though her fair hair and extremely light eyebrows gave her a frail and colorless appearance. Her eyes were deep blue and round, so that she always looked a little inquisitive, like a child to whom everything is new. "Did you say something, Mrs. Hamilton?"

"People don't change very much in a year, unless it's a bad year. And I haven't really had a bad year until this—until now."

The girl made a sympathetic sound, to which Mrs. Hamilton reacted stiffly. Mrs. Hamilton actively disliked and resented sympathy. In contrast to her plump small-boned body, her nature was

7

brisk and vigorous. Holding her large black purse firmly under her arm she crossed the swept concrete apron toward the entrance to the terminal. As she passed the ramp she glanced up at the vegetable-faces once more.

"I don't see Paul. Do you, Alice?"

"He might be waiting inside," the girl said. "It's cold."

"I told you to be sure and buy a warm enough coat."

"The coat's warm enough. But the wind isn't."

"Californians get spoiled. For winter this is quite balmy." But her own lips were blue-tinged, and her fingers inside the white doeskin gloves felt stiff as though they were in splints. "I didn't ask him to meet me in my telegram. Well, we'll take a taxi to Arbana. What time is it?"

"About nine."

"Too late. They probably won't let me see Virginia tonight."

"Probably not."

"I guess the—I guess *they* have visiting hours like a hospital." She spoke the word *they* as if it had an explosive content and must be handled carefully.

There was a line-up at the luggage counter, and they took their places at the end of it. To Mrs. Hamilton, who was quick to sense atmosphere, the big room had an air of excitement gone stale, anticipation soured by reality.

Journey's end, she thought. She felt stale and sour herself, and the feeling reminded her of Virginia; Virginia at Christmas time, the year she was eight. For weeks and weeks the child had dreamed of Christmas, and then on Christmas morning she had awakened and found that Christmas was only another day. There were presents, of course, but they weren't, they never could be, as big and exciting and mysterious as the packages they came in. In the afternoon Virginia had wept, rocking herself back and forth in misery.

8

"I want my Christmas back again. I want *my* Christmas!" Mrs. Hamilton knew now that what Virginia had wanted back were the wild and wonderful hopes, the boxes unopened, the ribbons still in bows.

Soon, in two weeks, there would be a new Christmas. She wondered, grimly, if Virginia would weep for its return when it was gone.

"You must be tired," Alice said. "Why don't you sit down and let me wait in line?"

The response was crisp and immediate. "No, thanks. I refuse to be treated like an old lady, at my age."

"Willett told me I was to be sure and look after you properly."

"My son Willett was born to be an old maid. I have no illusions about my children. Never had any. I know that Virginia is temperamental. But that's *all*. There's no harm in her." She rubbed her moist pallid forehead with a handkerchief. The room seemed unbearably hot, suddenly, and she was unbearably tired, but she felt impelled to go on talking. "The charge is false, preposterous. In a small town like Arbana the police are inefficient and probably corrupt. They've made an absurd mistake."

She had spoken the same words a dozen times in the past dozen hours. They had, with repetition, gained force and speed like a runaway car going downhill, heading for a crash.

"Wait until you meet her, Alice. You'll find out for yourself."

"I'm sure I will." Yet the more Mrs. Hamilton talked about Virginia, the more obscure Virginia became, hidden in a thicket of words like an unknown animal.

"I have no illusions," the older woman repeated. "She is temperamental, even bad-tempered at times, but she's incapable of injuring anyone deliberately."

Alice murmured an indistinct but reassuring answer. She had become conscious, suddenly, of being a focus of attention. She

9

turned and looked over Mrs. Hamilton's shoulder toward the exit door. A man was standing near the door watching her. He was in his middle thirties, tall, a little slouched as if he worked too long at a desk, and a little hard-faced, as if he didn't enjoy it. He wore a tweed topcoat that looked new, and a gray fedora and heavy brown English brogues.

"I think your son-in-law just came in."

Mrs. Hamilton turned too, and glanced brightly at the man. "That's not Paul. Too well-dressed. Paul always looks like someone in a soup line."

"He seems to know you, by the way he stares."

"Nonsense. Don't be so modest. He's staring at you. You're a pretty girl."

"I don't feel pretty."

"No woman *feels* pretty without a man. I used to feel pretty, though I never was, of course."

It was true. She had never been pretty even as a girl. Her head was too large for her body and emphasized by thick brown hair that was now burning itself out like a grass-fire and showing streaks of ashes. "You must learn to *pretend*, Alice. After all, you're not a schoolteacher any more. You're a young woman of the world, you're traveling, all sorts of exciting things can happen to you. Don't you feel that?"

"No," Alice said simply.

"Well, try."

The man at the door had come to a decision. He crossed the room briskly, removing his hat as he walked.

"Mrs. Hamilton?"

Mrs. Hamilton faced him, a slight frown creasing the skin between her eyebrows. The encounter, whatever it meant, wasn't in her plans. She had no time to waste or energy to squander on a stranger. She gripped her purse a little tighter as if the stranger had come to steal something from her.

"Yes, I'm Mrs. Hamilton."

"My name is Eric Meecham. Dr. Barkeley sent me to meet you."

"Oh. Well, how do you do?"

"How do you do?" He had a low-pitched voice with a faint rumble of impatience in it.

"You're a friend of Paul's?"

"No."

"Then?"

"I'm a lawyer. I've been retained to represent your daughter."

"Who hired you?"

"Dr. Barkeley."

"In my wire I instructed him to wait until I arrived."

Meecham returned her frown. "Well, he didn't. He wanted me to try and get her out of jail right away."

"And did you?"

"No."

"Why not? If it's money, I have…"

"It's not money. They can hold her for forty-eight hours without charge. It looks as if that's what they're going to do."

"But how can they hold an innocent girl?"

Meecham picked up the question carefully as if it was loaded. "The fact is, she hasn't claimed to be innocent."

"What—what does she claim?"

"Nothing. She won't deny anything, won't admit anything, won't, period. She's…" He groped for a word and out of the number that occurred to him he chose the least offensive: "She's a little difficult."

"She's frightened, the poor child. When she's frightened she's always difficult."

"I can see that." The line-up had dwindled down to just the three of them. Meecham looked questioningly at Alice, then turned back to Mrs. Hamilton. "You came alone?"

"No. No, I'm sorry, I forgot to introduce you. Alice, this is Mr. Meecham. Miss Dwyer."

Meecham nodded. "How do you do?"

"Alice is a friend of mine," Mrs. Hamilton explained.

"I'm a hired companion, really," Alice said.

"Really? If you'll give me the luggage checks, I'll get your things and take them out to my car."

Mrs. Hamilton handed him the checks. "It was kind of you to go to all this trouble."

"No trouble at all." The words were polite but without conviction.

He carried the four suitcases out to the car and piled them in the luggage compartment. The car was new but splattered with mud and there was a dent in the left rear fender.

The two women sat in the back and Meecham alone in the front. No one spoke for the first few miles. Traffic on the highway was heavy and the pavement slippery with slush.

Alice looked out at the countryside visible in the glare of headlights. It was bleak and flat, covered with patches of gray snow. A wave of homesickness swept over her, and mingled with it was a feeling much stronger and more violent than homesickness. She hated this place, and she hated the lawyer because he belonged to it. He was as crude and stark as the landscape and as ungracious as the weather.

Mrs. Hamilton seemed to share her feeling. She reached over suddenly and patted Alice's hand. Then she straightened up and addressed Meecham in her clear, deliberate voice: "Just what are your qualifications for this work, Mr. Meecham?"

"I took my law degree here at the University and played office boy to the firm of Post and Cranston until they found me indispensable and put my name on a door. Is that what you want to know?"

"I want to know what experience you've had with criminal cases."

"I've never handled a murder case, if that's what you mean," he said frankly. "They're not common around town. You know Arbana?"

"I've been there. Once."

"Then you know it's a university town and it hasn't a crime rate like Detroit's. The biggest policing problem is the traffic after football games. Naturally there's a certain percentage of auto thefts, robberies, morals offenses and things like that. But there hasn't been a murder for two years, until now."

"And they've arrested my daughter."

"Yes."

"I can't, I just can't believe it. All they had to do is take one look at Virginia to realize that she's a—a *nice* girl, well brought up."

"Nice girls have been in trouble before."

There was a brief silence. "You sound as if you think she's guilty."

"I've formed no opinion."

"You have. I can tell." Mrs. Hamilton leaned forward, one hand on the back of Meecham's seat. "Excuse me if I sound rude," she said softly, "but I'm not sure you're qualified to handle this business."

"I'm not sure either, but I'm going to try."

"Naturally you'll try. If murders are as rare in this town as you claim, it would be quite a feather in your cap to conduct a defense, wouldn't it?"

"It could be."

13

"I don't believe I'd like to see you wearing that feather, at my daughter's expense."

"What do you suggest that I do, Mrs. Hamilton?"

"Retire gracefully."

"I'm not graceful," Meecham said.

"I see. Well, I'll talk it over with Paul tonight."

They were approaching the town. There was a red neon glow in the sky and service stations and hamburger stands appeared at shorter intervals along the highway.

Mrs. Hamilton spoke again. "It's not that I have anything against you personally, Mr. Meecham."

"No."

"It's just that my daughter is the most important thing in my life. I can't take any chances."

Meecham thought of a dozen retorts, but he didn't make any of them. He felt genuinely sorry for the woman, or for anyone to whom Virginia Barkeley was the most important thing in life.

TWO

One wing of the house was dark, but in the other wing lights streamed from every window like golden ribbons.

The place was larger than Meecham had expected, and its flat roof and enormous windows looked incongruous in a winter setting. It was a Southern California house, of redwood and fieldstone. Meecham wondered whether Virginia had planned it that way herself, deliberately, because it reminded her of home, or unconsciously, as a symbol of her own refusal to conform to a new environment.

The driveway entrance to the house was through a patio that separated the two wings. Here, too, the lights were on, revealing hanging baskets of dead plants and flowerpots heaped with snow, and a barbecue pit fringed with tiny icicles.

Mrs. Hamilton's eyes were squinted up as if she was going to cry at the sight of Virginia's patio, built for sun and summer and now desolate in the winter night. Silently she got out of the car and moved toward the house.

Meecham pushed back his hat in a gesture of relief. "Quite a character, eh?"

"I like her. She's very pleasant to me."

"Oh?" He stood aside while Alice stepped out of the car. "You're a little young to be a hired companion. How long have you worked for her?"

"About a month."

"Why?"

"Why? Well…" She flushed again. "Well, that's a silly question. I have to earn a living."

"I meant, it's a funny kind of job for a young girl."

"I used to be a schoolteacher. Only I wasn't meeting…" *any eligible men* were the words that occurred to her, but she said instead, "I was getting into a rut, so I decided to change jobs for a year or so."

He gave her a queer look and went around to the back of the car to unlock the luggage compartment. Mrs. Hamilton had gone into the house, leaving the front door open.

Meecham put the four suitcases on the shoveled drive and relocked the compartment. "I suppose you know what you're getting into."

"I—of course. *Naturally*."

"Naturally." He looked slightly amused. "I gather you haven't met Virginia."

"No. I've heard a lot about her, though, from her brother, Willett, and from Mrs. Hamilton. She seems to be—well, rather an unhappy person."

"You have to be pretty unhappy," Meecham said, "to stab a guy half a dozen times in the neck. Or didn't you know about that?"

"I knew it." She meant to sound very positive, like Mrs. Hamilton, but her voice was squeezed into a tight little whisper. "Of course I knew it."

"Naturally."

"You're quite objectionable."

"I am when people object to me," Meecham said. "I've forgotten your name, by the way, what is it?"

Instead of answering she picked up two of the suitcases and went ahead into the house.

Mrs. Hamilton heard her coming and called out, "Alice? I'm here, in the living room. Bring Mr. Meecham in with you. Perhaps he'd like some coffee."

Alice looked coldly at Meecham who had followed her in. "Would you like some coffee?"

"No, thanks, *Alice.*"

"I don't permit total strangers to call me Alice."

"Okay, kid." He looked as if he was going to laugh, but he didn't. Instead, he said, "We seem to have started off on the wrong foot."

"Since we're not going anywhere together, what does it matter?"

"Have it your way." He put on his hat. "Tell Mrs. Hamilton I'll meet her tomorrow morning at 9:30 at the county jail. She can see Virginia then."

"Couldn't she phone her tonight or something?"

"The girl's in jail. She's not staying at the Waldorf." He said over his shoulder as he went out the door, "Good night, kid."

"Alice?" Mrs. Hamilton repeated. "Oh, there you are. Where's Mr. Meecham?"

"He left."

"Perhaps I was a little harsh with him, challenging his abilities." She was standing in front of the fireplace, still in her hat and coat, and rubbing her hands together as if to get warm, though the fire wasn't lit. "I'm afraid I antagonized him. I couldn't help it. I felt he had the wrong attitude toward Virginia."

The room was very large and colorful, furnished in rattan and bamboo and glass like a tropical lanai. There were growing plants everywhere, philodendron and ivy hanging from copper planters on the walls, azaleas in tubs, and cyclamen and coleus and saint-paulia in bright coralstone pots on the mantel and on every shelf and table. The air was humid and smelled of moist earth like a field after a spring rain.

The whole effect of the room was one of impossible beauty and excess, as if the person who lived there lived in a dream.

"She loves flowers," Mrs. Hamilton said. "She isn't like Willett, my son. He's never cared for anything except money. But Virginia is quite different. Even when she was a child she was always very gentle with flowers as she was with birds and animals. Very gentle and understanding…"

"Mrs. Hamilton."

"…as if they were people and could feel."

"Mrs. Hamilton," Alice repeated, and the woman blinked as if just waking up. "Why is Virginia in jail? What did she do?"

She was fully awake now, the questions had struck her vulnerable body as hailstones strike a field of sun-warmed wheat. "Virginia didn't do anything. She was arrested by mistake."

"But why?"

"I've told you, Paul's wire to me was very brief. I know none of the details."

"You could have asked Mr. Meecham."

"I prefer to get the details from someone closer to me and to Virginia."

She doesn't want the facts at all, Alice thought. All she wants is to have Virginia back again, the gentle child who loved animals and flowers.

A middle-aged woman in horn-rimmed glasses and a white uniform came into the room carrying a cup of coffee, half of which had spilled into the saucer. She had a limp but she moved very quickly as if she thought speed would cover it. She had a spot of color on each cheekbone, round as coins.

"Here you are. This'll warm you up." She spoke a little too loudly, covering her embarrassment with volume as she covered her limp with speed.

Mrs. Hamilton nodded her thanks. "Carney, this is Alice Dwyer. Alice, Mrs. Carnova."

The woman shook Alice's hand vigorously. "Call me Carney. Everyone does."

"Carney," Mrs. Hamilton explained, "is Paul's office nurse, and an old friend of mine."

"He phoned from the hospital a few minutes ago. He's on his way."

"We are old friends, aren't we, Carney?"

The coins on the woman's cheekbones expanded. "Sure. You bet we are."

"Then what are you acting so nervous about?"

"Nervous? Well, everybody gets nervous once in a while, don't they? I've had a busy day and I stayed after hours to welcome you, see that you got settled, and so forth. I'm tired, is all."

"Is it?"

The two women had forgotten Alice. Carney was looking down at the floor, and the color had radiated all over her face to the tops of her large pale ears. "Why did you come? You can't do anything."

"I can. I'm going to."

"You don't know how things are."

"Then tell me."

"This is bad, the worst yet. I knew she was seeing Margolis. I warned her. I said I'd write and tell you and you'd come and make it hot for her."

"You didn't tell me."

Carney spread her hands. "How could I? She's twenty-six; that's too old to be kept in line by threats of telling mama."

"Did Paul know about this—this man?"

"I'm not sure. Maybe he did. He never said anything." She plucked a dried leaf from the yam plant that was growing down from the mantel. "Virginia won't listen to me any more. She doesn't like me."

"That's silly. She's always been devoted to you."

"Not any more. Last week she called me a snooping old beer-hound. She said that when I applied for this job it wasn't because Carnova had left me stranded in Detroit, it was because you sent me here to spy on her."

"That's ridiculous," Mrs. Hamilton said crisply. "I'll talk to Virginia tomorrow and see that she apologizes."

"*Apologizes.* What do you think this is, some little *game* or something? Oh, God." Carney exploded. She covered her face with her hands, half-laughing, half-crying and then she began to hiccough, loud and fast. "Oh—damn—oh—damn."

Mrs. Hamilton turned to Alice. "We all need some rest. Come and I'll show you your room."

"I'll—show—her."

"All right. You go with Carney, Alice. I'll wait up to say hello to Paul."

Alice looked embarrassed. "I hated to stand there listening like that. About Virginia, I mean."

"That's all right, you couldn't help it." A car came up the driveway and stopped with a shriek of brakes. "Here's Paul now. I'll talk to him alone, Carney, if you don't mind."

"Why—should—I—mind?"

"And for heaven's sake breathe into a paper bag or something. Good night."

When they had gone Mrs. Hamilton stood in the center of the room for a moment, her fingertips pressing her temples, her eyes closed. She felt exhausted, not from the sleepless night she had spent, or from the plane trip, but from the strain of uncertainty, and the more terrible strain of pretending that everything would be all right, that a mistake had been made which could be rather easily corrected.

She went to open the door for Paul.

He came in, stamping the snow from his boots, a stocky, power-fully built man in a wrinkled trench coat and a damp shapeless gray hat. He looked like a red-cheeked farmer coming in from his evening's chores, carrying a medical bag instead of a lantern.

He had a folded newspaper under his arm. Mrs. Hamilton glanced at the newspaper and away again.

"Well, Paul." They shook hands briefly.

"I'm glad you got here all right." He had a very deep warm voice and he talked rather slowly, weighing out each word with care like a prescription. "Sorry I couldn't meet you—Mother."

"You don't have to call me Mother, you know, if it makes you uncomfortable."

"Then I won't." He laid his hat and trench coat across a chair and put his medical bag on top of them. But he kept the newspaper in his hand, rolling it up very tight as if he intended to use it as a weapon, to swat a fly or discipline an unruly pup.

Mrs. Hamilton sat down suddenly and heavily, as though the newspaper had been used against her. The light from the rattan lamp struck her face with the sharpness of a slap. "That paper you have, what is it?"

"One of the Detroit tabloids."

"Is it…?"

"It's all in here, yes. Not on the front page."

"Are there any pictures?"

"Yes."

"Of Virginia?"

"One."

"Let me see."

"It's not very pretty," he said. "Perhaps you'd better not."

"I must see it."

"All right."

The pictures occupied the entire second page. There were three of them. One, captioned DEATH SHACK, showed a small cottage, its roof heavy with fresh snow and its windows opaque with frost. The second was of a sleek dark-haired man smiling into the camera. He was identified as Claude Ross Margolis, forty-two, prominent contractor, victim of fatal stabbing.

The third picture was of Virginia, though no one would have recognized her. She was sitting on some kind of bench, hunched over, with her hands covering her face and a tangled mass of black hair falling over her wrists. She wore evening slippers, one of them minus a heel, and a long fluffy dress and light-colored coat. The coat and dress and one of the shoes showed dark stains that looked like mud. Above the picture were the words, *held for questioning*, and underneath it Virginia was identified as Mrs. Paul Barkeley, twenty-six, wife of Arbana physician, allegedly implicated in the death of Claude Margolis.

Mrs. Hamilton spoke finally in a thin, ragged whisper: "I've seen a thousand such dreary pictures in my life, but I never thought that some day one of them would be terribly different to me from all the others."

She looked up at Barkeley. His face hadn't changed expression, it showed no sign of awareness that the girl in the picture was his wife. A little pulse of resentment began to beat in the back of Mrs. Hamilton's mind: *He doesn't care—he should have taken better care of Virginia—this would never have happened. Why wasn't he with her? Or why didn't he keep her at home?*

She said, not trying to hide her resentment, "Where were you when it happened, Paul?"

"Right here at home. In bed."

"You knew she was out."

"She'd been going out a great deal lately."

22

"Didn't you care?"

"Of course I cared. Unfortunately, I have to make a living. I can't afford to follow Virginia around picking up the pieces." He went over to the built-in bar in the south corner of the room. "Have a nightcap with me."

"No, thanks. I—those stains on her clothes, they're blood?"

"Yes."

"Whose blood?"

"His. Margolis'."

"How can they tell?"

"There are lab tests to determine whether blood is human and what type it is."

"Well. Well, anyway, I'm glad it's not hers." She hesitated, glancing at the paper and away again, as if she would have liked to read the report for herself but was afraid to. "She wasn't hurt?"

"No. She was drunk."

Drunk?"

"Yes." He poured some bourbon into a glass and added water. Then he held the glass up to the light as if he was searching for microbes in a test tube. "A police patrol car picked her up. They found her wandering around about a quarter of a mile from Margolis' cottage. It was snowing very hard; she must have lost her way."

"Wandering around in the snow with only that light coat and those thin shoes—oh God, I can't bear it."

"You'll have to," he said quietly. "Virginia's depending on you."

"I know, I know she is. Tell me—the rest."

"There isn't much. Margolis' body had been discovered by that time because something had gone wrong with the fireplace in the cottage. There was a lot of smoke, someone reported it, and the highway patrol found Margolis inside dead, stabbed with his own knife. He'd been living in the cottage which is just outside the city limits because his own house was closed. His wife is in Peru on a holiday."

"His wife. He was married."

"Yes."

"There were—children?"

"Two."

"Drunk," Mrs. Hamilton whispered. "And out with a married man. There must be some mistake, surely, surely there is."

"No. I saw her myself. The Sheriff called me about three o'clock this morning and told me she was being held and why. I wired you immediately, and then I went down to the county jail where they'd taken her. She was still drunk, didn't even recognize me. Or pretended not to. How can you tell, with Virginia, what's real and what isn't?"

"*I* can tell."

"Can you?" He sipped at his drink. "The sheriff and a couple of deputies were there trying to get a statement from her. They didn't get one, of course. I told them it was silly to go on questioning anyone in her condition, so they let her go back to bed."

"In a cell? With thieves and prostitutes and…"

"She was alone. The cell—*room*, rather, was clean. I saw it. And the matron, or deputy, I think they called her, seemed a decent young woman. The surroundings aren't quite what Virginia is used to, but she's not suffering. Don't worry about that part of it."

"You don't appear to be worrying at all."

"I've done nothing but worry, for a long time." He hesitated, looking at her across the room as if wondering how much of the truth she wanted to hear. "You may as well know now—Virginia will tell you, if I don't—that this first year of our marriage has been bad. The worst year of my life, and maybe the worst in Virginia's too."

Mrs. Hamilton's face looked crushed, like paper in a fist. "Why didn't someone *tell* me? Virginia wrote to me, Carney wrote. No one said anything. I thought things were going well, that Virginia had settled down with you and was happy, that she was finally happy. Now I find out I've been deceived. She didn't settle down. She's been running around with married men, getting drunk, behaving like a cheap tart. And now this, this final disgrace. I just don't know what to *do*, what to *think*."

He saw the question in her eyes, and turned away, holding his glass up to the light again.

"I did what I could, hired a lawyer."

"Yes, but what kind? A man with no experience."

"He was recommended to me."

"He's not good enough. Virginia should have the best."

"She should indeed," he said dryly. "Unfortunately, I can't afford the best."

"I can. Money is no object."

"That money-is-no-object idea is a little old-fashioned, I'm afraid." He put down his empty glass. "There's another point. If Virginia is innocent, she won't need the best. Now if you'll excuse me, I think I'll go to bed. I have to keep early hours. Carney showed you your room, I suppose?"

"Yes."

"Make yourself at home as much as possible. The house is yours," he added with a wry little smile. "Mortgage and all. Good night, Mrs. Hamilton."

"Good night." She hesitated for a split second before adding, "my boy."

He went out of the room. She followed him with her eyes; they were perfectly dry now, and hard and gray as granite.

Red-faced farmer, she thought viciously.

THREE

In the summer the red bricks of the courthouse were covered with dirty ivy and in the winter with dirty snow. The building had been constructed on a large square in what was originally the center of town. But the town had moved westward, abandoned the courthouse like an ugly stepchild, leaving it in the east end to fend for itself among the furniture warehouses and service stations and beer-and-sandwich cafés.

Across the road from the main entrance was a supermarket. Meecham parked his car in front of it. Its doors were still closed, though there was activity inside. Along the aisles clerks moved apathetically, slowed by sleep and the depression of a winter morning that was no different from night. Street lamps were still burning, the sky was dark, the air heavy and damp.

Meecham crossed the road. He felt sluggish, and wished he could have stayed in bed until it was light.

In front of the courthouse a thirty-foot Christmas tree had been put up and four county prisoners were stringing it with colored lights under the direction of a deputy. The deputy wore fuzzy orange ear-muffs, and he kept stamping his feet rhythmically, either to keep warm or because there was nothing else to do.

When Meecham approached, all four of the prisoners stopped work to look at him, as they stopped to look at nearly everyone who passed, realizing that they had plenty of time and nothing to lose by a delay.

"Speed it up a little, eh, fellows?" The deputy whacked his hands together. "What's the matter, you paralyzed or something, Joe?"

Joe looked down from the top of the ladder and laughed, showing his upper teeth filled at the gum-line with gold. "How'd you like to be inside with a nice rum toddy, Huggins? Mmm?"

"I never touch the stuff," Huggins said. "Morning, Meecham."

Meecham nodded. "Morning."

"Up early catching worms?"

"That's right."

Huggins jerked his thumb at the ladder. "Me, I'm trying to inject the spirit of Christmas into these bums."

Three of the men laughed. The fourth spat into the snow.

Meecham went inside. The steam had been turned on full force and the old-fashioned radiators were clanking like ghosts rattling their chains. Meecham was sweating before he reached the middle of the corridor, and the passages from his nose to his throat felt hot and dry as if he'd been breathing fire.

The main corridor smelled of wood and fresh wax, but when he descended the stairs on the left a new smell rose to overpower the others, the smell of disinfectant.

The door lettered County Sheriff was open. Meecham walked into the anteroom and sat down in one of the straight chairs that were lined up against the wall like mute and motionless prisoners. The anteroom was empty, though a man's coat and hat were hanging on a rack in the corner, and the final inch of a cigarette was smoldering in an ash tray on the scarred wooden counter. Meecham looked at the cigarette but made no move to put it out.

The door of the Sheriff's private office banged open suddenly and Cordwink himself came out. He was a tall man, match-thin, with gray hair that was clipped short to disguise its curl. His eyelashes curled too, giving his cold eyes a false appearance of naivete. He had fifty years of hard living behind him, but they didn't show except when he was tired or when he'd had a quarrel with his wife over money or one of the kids.

"What are you doing around so early?" Cordwink said.

"I wanted to be the first to wish you a Merry Christmas."

"You bright young lawyers, you keep me all the time in stitches. Yah." He scowled at the cigarette smoldering in the ash tray. "What the hell you trying to do, burn the place down?"

"It's not my..."

"That's about the only way you'll get your client out of here."

"Oh?" Meecham lit a cigarette and used the burnt match to crush out the burning remnants of tobacco in the ash tray. "Have you dug up any new information?"

"I should tell you?" Cordwink laughed. "You bloody lawyers can do your own sleuthing."

"Kind of sour this morning, aren't you, Sheriff?"

"I'm in a sour business, I meet sour people, so I'm sour. So?"

"So you didn't get a statement from Mrs. Barkeley."

"Sure I got a statement."

"Such as?"

"Such as that I'm an illiterate buffoon of canine parentage." Meecham grinned.

"That strikes you as humorous, eh, Meecham?"

"Moderately."

"Well, it so happens that I graduated from the University of Wisconsin, class of '22."

"Funny, I thought you were a Harvard man. You act and talk like a..."

"You bright young lawyers kill me." He grunted. "Yah. Well, I don't care if she makes a statement or not. We have her."

"Maybe."

"Even you ought to be smart enough to see that. You'd better start combing the books for some fancy self-defense items. Make sure you get a nice stupid jury, then razz the cops, turn on the tears, quote the Bible—yah! Makes me sick. What a way to make a living, obstructing justice."

"I've heard the theme song before, Sheriff. Let's skip the second chorus."

"You think I'm off-key, eh?"

"Sure you are."

Cordwink pressed a buzzer on the counter. "You won't get away with a self-defense plea. There isn't a mark on the girl, no cut, no bruise, not a scratch."

"I don't have to prove that the danger to her person was objectively real and imminent, only that she thought, and had reason to think, that it was real and imminent."

"You're not in court yet, so can the jargon. Makes me sick."

The Sheriff pressed the buzzer again and a moment later a young woman in a green dress came into the room blithely swinging a ring of keys.

She greeted Meecham with a show of fine white teeth. "You again, Mr. Meecham."

"Right."

"You ought to just move in." She switched the smile on Cordwink. "Isn't that right, Sheriff?"

"Righter than you think," Cordwink said. "If justice was done, the place would be crawling with lawyers." He started toward his office. "Show the gentleman into Mrs. Barkeley's boudoir, Miss Jennings."

"Okeydoke." Cordwink slammed his door and Miss Jennings added, in a stage whisper, "My, aren't we short-tempered this morning."

"Must be the weather."

"You know, I think it is, Mr. Meecham. Personally, the weather never bothers me. I rise above it. When winter comes can spring be far behind?"

"You have something there."

"Shakespeare. I adore poetry."

"Good, good." He followed her down the corridor. "How is Mrs. Barkeley?"

"She had a good sleep and a big breakfast. I think she's finally over her hangover. My, it was a beaut." She unlocked the door at the end of the corridor and held it open for Meecham to go through first. "She borrowed my lipstick. That's a good sign."

"Maybe. But I don't know of what."

"Oh, you're just cynical. So many people are cynical. My mother often says to me, Mollie dear, you were born smiling and you'll probably go out smiling."

Meecham shuddered. "Lucky girl."

"Yes, I am lucky. I simply can't *help* looking at the cheerful side."

"Good for you."

The women's section of the cell-block was empty except for Virginia. Miss Jennings unlocked the door. "Here's that man again, Mrs. Barkeley."

Virginia was sitting on her narrow cot reading, or pretending to read, a magazine. She was wearing the yellow wool dress and brown sandals that Meecham had brought to her the previous afternoon, and her black hair was brushed carefully back from her high forehead. She had used Miss Jennings' lipstick to advantage, painting her mouth fuller and wider than it actually was. In the light of the single overhead bulb her flesh looked smooth and cold as marble. Meecham found it impossible to imagine what emotions she was feeling, or what was going on behind her remote and beautiful eyes.

She raised her head and gave him a long unfriendly stare that reminded him of Mrs. Hamilton, though there was no physical resemblance between the mother and daughter.

"Good morning, Mrs. Barkeley."

"Why don't you get me out of here?" she said flatly.

"I'm trying."

He stepped inside and Miss Jennings closed the door behind him but didn't lock it. She retired to the end of the room and sat down on a bench near the exit door. She hummed a few bars of music, very casually, to indicate to Meecham and Virginia that she had no intention of eavesdropping. *I'll take the high road...*

"She sings," Virginia said. "She whistles. She quoted poetry. She's so cheerful it drives me crazy. You've got to get me *out* of here."

"I'm trying."

"You said that before."

"Now I'm repeating it. Mind if I sit down?"

"I don't care."

He sat down at the foot of the cot. "How's your hangover?"

"It's all right. But they've got fleas or something in here. I have more of those red welts all over my ankles. Did you remember to bring the DDT?"

"Sure." He took the small bottle of DDT out of his overcoat pocket and gave it to her.

She read the label, frowning. "It's only two percent."

"I couldn't get it any stronger."

"You could."

"All right, but I didn't."

"What were you afraid of, that I'd drink it in remorse or something?"

"It occurred to me," Meecham said. "Now don't get excited. Your mother will be here soon."

"When?"

"Nine-thirty."

"Do I—do I look all right?"

"You look fine. Very pretty, in fact."

"Don't say that. I know I'm not pretty."

Meecham smiled. "We disagree about so many things, let's not disagree about that. Where did you get the cockeyed idea that you're not pretty?"

"I know I'm not. We won't discuss it."

"All right." He offered her a cigarette and she shook her head in refusal. "Let's discuss Cordwink. Give him a statement today and you'll be out…"

"I wouldn't give him the time of day."

"Why not?"

Her lips tightened. "I know what I'm doing. If I refuse to tell Cordwink anything, he won't have anything to trip me up with later on."

"That argument is sound but rather limited."

"Besides, now that my mother's here, she'll handle everything."

"Oh?"

"Wait and see."

"Your mother," Meecham said dryly, "is undoubtedly a strong and persevering woman, but she can't handle an entire sheriff's department."

She looked at him stubbornly. "She *believes* in me."

"I don't care if she thinks you're Queen of the May, a mother's faith isn't enough to go to court on."

"I won't be going to court."

"No?"

"I'm not guilty. I didn't kill him." She raised her voice. "Hear that, Miss Big Ears? I didn't kill Margolis."

Miss Jennings began to hum again: *And you'll take the low road.*

"Well, that's something anyway," Meecham said. "A denial. Can you back it up?"

"That's all I'm saying right now."

"Why?"

"Because it *is*."

"Because you don't remember," Meecham said. "According to the lab report your blood alcohol was 2.23."

"What does that mean?"

"You were loaded."

Virginia's cheeks turned slightly pink. "Does my mother know that?"

"She must, by this time."

"She'll be furious. She's a teetotaler." She said it very seriously, as if the crime of which she was accused was not murder but drinking.

"So you won't give Cordwink a statement."

"I can't. Don't you understand? I can't tell him I don't remember anything, he'll throw the book at me."

"He may anyway."

She bit her lower lip. "I admit I was a little high Saturday night."

"You were quite stupendously drunk, Mrs. Barkeley. You weren't a little high."

"Well, stop repeating it!" she cried. "Why did you come here anyway? I don't need you to tell me what to do."

"Don't you?"

There was a pause. Miss Jennings was wide-eyed with curiosity, but she hummed valiantly on, keeping time with her left foot.

"You weren't drunk all Saturday night. What happened earlier, before Margolis was killed?"

"We danced and had something to eat."

"You also had a fight around eleven o'clock."

"Claude and I were the best of friends," she said stiffly.

"It's on the record, Mrs. Barkeley. A waitress at the Top Hat remembers you both and has already identified your pictures. In the middle of the argument you got up and walked out and a few minutes later Margolis followed you. Where did you go? Or don't you want me to tell you?"

"You like talking so much, tell me." The words were arrogant, but they weren't spoken arrogantly. Her voice trembled, and Meecham wondered if she was frightened at the thought of meeting her mother. She had shown no previous signs of fear.

He said, "You went to a beer-and-pretzel place a couple of doors down the street. It was jammed with the Saturday-night college crowd. Margolis caught up with you there. You were at the bar talking to a man when Margolis arrived. You got up and left with Margolis, and the other man got up and left too, according to one of the bartenders. But he doesn't know whether the man left with you, or whether he was just going home because it was nearly closing time. Which was it?"

"Stop." Virginia pounded the edge of the cot with her fist. "Do we have to go into it like this?"

"Somebody has to. We can't all sit around nursing our amnesia."

"You're pretty insolent, for hired help."

"And you're pretty uncooperative for a girl who might spend her next twenty years sorting out dirty clothes in a prison laundry."

"That was an ugly remark." The girl's face was paper-white, and her skin seemed to be stretched tight and transparent across her cheekbones. "I won't forget it."

"I hope not," Meecham said. "There's one very interesting point about the finding of Margolis' body. His wallet was missing."

"What difference does that make?"

"His friends claim he always carried a fair amount of cash."

"He did."

"It makes me wonder about your anonymous stranger at the bar. I gather you didn't take Margolis' wallet?"

"Why should I?"

"Because you're broke."

"So you've been checking up. Afraid you're not going to get paid?"

"I've been checking. Your car isn't paid for, your house is mortgaged, your husband is..."

"Leave Paul out of this," she said sharply. "And get one thing straight—if I want money, I don't have to go around lifting wallets."

"You can ask your mother."

"That's right, I can."

"Well, here's your chance." Meecham glanced at his watch. "She should be arriving right now."

The overhead lights went off suddenly and the feeble rays of the morning sun filtered in through the barred windows like dim hopes.

Virginia got up and looked out the window at her little square of sky. "I can't see her in here. There must be some other place."

"I'll see what I can do." He opened the cell door and stepped out. "Miss Jennings?"

Miss Jennings came up, swinging her keys. "All through for now?"

"Mrs. Barkeley's mother is coming to visit her. They haven't seen each other for a year. I thought we might be able to borrow some other room for a while, Miss Jennings."

"Well, I guess so. I'll see. After all, one's own *mother.*" She glanced rather uncertainly at Virginia. "I'll have to stay with you all the time. Mr. Meecham can talk to you in private because he's your lawyer. But anyone else... There are rules, even about mothers."

"What do you think she's going to do," Virginia said, "slip me a loaf of bread with a chisel inside?"

Miss Jennings laughed hollowly. "She's a great one for joking, isn't she, Mr. Meecham?"

"Just great." He gave Virginia a warning glance and she went and sat down on the cot again with her back to them both.

Miss Jennings locked the cell door. "I'll go and ask the Sheriff if you can use his private office. But I don't guarantee a thing. He's not at his best this morning."

"Thanks for trying, anyway." When Miss Jennings had gone, he spoke through the bars to Virginia: "It's time you started to win friends and influence people."

"Really?"

"Put on an act. You're an innocent flower, dirt has been done by you, and now your dear old mother has come to visit you from the faraway hills."

"What ham. It's too thick to slice."

"Ham or not, try some," Meecham said. "By the way, do you know Margolis' wife?"

"I've met her. She has a bad complexion."

"How did you meet her?"

"That's none of your business."

"Everything about you is my business until you get out of here for good. How did you meet Margolis?"

"He built the house for me. For me and Paul, that is."

Miss Jennings returned and opened the cell door again. "Your mother's waiting in the Sheriff's office, Mrs. Barkeley. My, she doesn't resemble you a bit, except maybe just around the eyes. Family resemblances fascinate me. Here, you can borrow my compact mirror to see how you look."

"I know how I look," Virginia said.

"Now, is that nice?" Smiling cheerfully, Miss Jennings replaced the compact in her pocket. "You look sulky, if you want the truth."

Virginia opened her mouth to reply, caught another warning glance from Meecham and changed her mind. She followed Miss Jennings silently down the hall. Her face was calm, almost stony, but she walked as if she had trouble keeping her balance.

"Do you want me to stay?" Meecham asked.

Virginia half-turned and said, over her shoulder, "What for?"

"Well, there's my answer."

"Right."

He dropped behind the two women. When they reached the Sheriff's office Virginia went in ahead, taking little running steps. "Momma! *Momma!*"

Meecham wondered grimly whether this was the real thing or whether it was ham too thick to slice.

He walked slowly past the open door. Mrs. Hamilton was holding Virginia in her arms, rocking back and forth in grief and gladness. She was crying, and Virginia was crying, and Miss Jennings' face was all squeezed up as if she too was going to cry. All three of them looked so funny that for an instant Meecham almost laughed.

The instant passed.

"Ginny darling. Darling girl."

Christ, Meecham thought, and walked away as fast as possible to get out of earshot.

At the bottom of the stairs leading up to the main floor a man was sitting on a bench, his back resting against the wall.

Meecham stared at him curiously as he passed, and the man returned the stare, unselfconsciously, like someone accustomed to attracting attention. In spite of the winter weather he wore no coat or hat, and his skin was mushroom-pale as if he had lived underground for a long time, out of reach of the sun. He was still young. His face looked younger than Meecham's, but the shape of his body was like that of a dissolute old man—scrawny shoulders and pipestem wrists and a huge pendulous belly which he tried to hide by keeping his arms folded in front of him.

He looked at Meecham, his eyes enormous in the thin sensitive face, and then he rose heavily and awkwardly like a woman far gone with child and moved on down the corridor.

Meecham went up the stairs. Outside, the Christmas tree lights were in place and turned on, but they didn't show up very well because the sun was shining.

FOUR

When Meecham arrived at the house it was almost dark and snow was falling again, a fine light snow, iridescent, like crushed diamonds.

Alice met him at the door. Though he'd only seen her once before, on the previous night, she looked very familiar to him, like a kid sister. He glanced down at her with a critical brotherly eye. She was wearing a cherry-colored dress that didn't suit her; the lines were too straight, the color too vivid.

"Do I come in?" Meecham said.

"Well, I guess so."

"What's the matter? Anything wrong?"

"No. Except that there's no one here but me. Dr. Barkeley and Mrs. Hamilton are out."

"That's all right. Maybe I'm early."

"Early?"

"I was invited for tea." He consulted his watch. "At five. It's now five."

"No one told me anything about it. Mrs. Hamilton's been gone all day."

He took off his coat and laid it across a chair while Alice watched him, still looking puzzled and rather unfriendly.

She said, "Why did she invite you for tea?"

"Maybe she wants to read my tea leaves. That should be interesting," he added with a dry smile. "I might be about to get some money or meet a short suspicious blonde."

"That's not very funny."

"Then stop acting suspicious."

"I'm not."

"Have it your way."

He crossed the room and stood with his back to the mantel, his left arm supporting some of his weight. His body was never quite erect. When he walked he slouched, and when he stood he always leaned against something like a man who had spent too much time in a car and at a desk.

"Where is she?" he asked.

"At the movies. She phoned at noon and told me she intended to stay downtown for lunch and do some shopping and take in a double feature. She sounded quite gay and girlish, as if she was going on a spree."

"Maybe she was."

"Oh, no. She doesn't drink."

"I wasn't thinking of that kind of a spree."

"Then why don't you say what you think?"

"Maybe I will, sometime."

"I can hardly wait."

"Now what are you miffed about?"

"You're so condescending."

"I don't feel that way," he said gravely. "In fact, right now I'm confused. I can go down to lower Fifth Street and look in the window of a house, any house, and tell you quite a lot about the people who live there. But I'm not used to houses like this or girls like Virginia or women like Mrs. Hamilton."

"Or like me?" The question slipped out unintentionally, like a line from a fishing reel left unguarded for a moment.

"I think I know quite a bit about you, Alice."

"Oh? You've met dozens like me, I suppose."

"A few."

She turned away so that he couldn't see the angry flush that stained her face.

40

He didn't see it, though he guessed it was there. "Why does that make you mad?"

"I'm not mad."

"You wouldn't want to be absolutely unique, would you, like a three-headed calf or something?"

"Of course not." I would, she thought violently. I want to be absolutely unique.

"I'm sorry if I offended you," he said with a trace of a smile. "It's just that I knew a three-headed calf once, and all it ever wanted to be was ordinary."

"This is a ridiculous conversation," Alice said. "I think you'd better stick to looking in windows on lower Fifth Street, Mr. Meecham."

"I *don't* look in…"

"You said you did."

"I said I *could*."

"Anybody can. You hardly need any special equipment for window peeping."

"I am *not* a window peeper."

"Well, you said you were."

"I did not say I…"

"I heard you distinctly."

Meecham shook his head in exasperation. "All right. All right, I'm a window peeper."

"I can believe it."

"I think I've changed my mind about you, Alice. You *are* unique. Absolutely unique and impossible."

Alice gazed at him blandly. "I'd rather be impossible than ordinary. Mrs. Hamilton says I can be anything if I try."

"Mrs. Hamilton's an authority?"

"On most things."

"I wouldn't be too sure," he said. "Don't get stuck on the old girl. She might let you down."

From outside there came the sound of footsteps hurrying across the patio. A moment later the front door burst open and Mrs. Hamilton came rushing into the room. Her coat was flying open and her hat had slid to the back of her head. She looked blowsy and old and scared.

As she turned to close the door behind her the parcels she was carrying slid out of her arms and dropped to the floor. There was a muffled shatter of glass, and almost instantly the smell of lilacs crept poignantly into the room like a remembered spring.

"Turn off the lights, Alice," she said. "Don't ask questions. Turn them off."

Alice did as she was told. Without lights the smell of lilacs seemed stronger, and Mrs. Hamilton's harsh breathing rose and fell in the darkness.

"Someone is out there. A man. He's been following me."

Meecham coughed, faintly. She took it as a sign of disbelief.

"No, I'm not imagining things, Mr. Meecham," she said sharply. "He followed me from the bus stop. I couldn't get a cab downtown so I took the bus. This man got off at the same corner as I did. He followed me. I think he meant to rob me."

"He may live in one of the houses around here," Meecham said.

"No. He came after me quite deliberately and openly. When I walked fast he walked fast, and when I paused he paused. There was something almost sadistic about it."

"He's probably a neighborhood nut who gets his kicks out of scaring women," Meecham said. Or a policeman, he thought, maybe one of Cordwink's men. "Where is he now?"

"The last I saw of him he had gone behind the cedar hedge."

She crossed to the window and pointed. "Right there, at the entrance to the driveway. He might be there yet."

"I'll go out and take a look."

"What if he's dangerous? Maybe we should call the police immediately."

"First, let's see if he's still there," Meecham said.

Outside, the snow was still falling. It felt good, after the heat of the house. Through the patio and down the driveway Meecham walked, a little self-consciously, aware that the two women were watching him from the window and not sure how far they could see, since it wasn't totally dark yet.

By the time he reached the end of the curving driveway the snow didn't feel quite so pleasant. With quiet persistence it had seeped in over the tops of his shoes, and up his coat sleeves and down under his collar. He felt cold and wet and foolish.

He said, in a voice that wasn't as loud or as firm as he intended: "Hey. You behind the hedge. What are you doing?"

There was no answer. He had expected none. The old girl had probably dreamed up the whole thing. Darkness, weariness, a deserted street, footsteps behind—together they were rich food for the imagination.

Pulling up his coat collar against the snow, he was on the point of turning to go back to the house when a man shuffled out from the shadow of the hedge. He moved like an old man, and his hair and eyebrows were white, but the whiteness was snow. He stood with his back to the street lamp so that his face was just a blur in the deepening twilight. The light-colored baggy coat he wore hung on him like a tent.

"What am I doing here?" he said. "I'm waiting for the doctor."

"Behind a hedge?"

"No, sir." He had a rather high, earnest voice, like a schoolboy's.

43

"I intend to go to his office, but I thought I'd stand here a bit and enjoy the night. I like a winter night."

"Kind of cold, isn't it?"

"Not for me. I like the smell of cedar too. It reminds me of Christmas. I won't be having a Christmas this year." He brushed the snow from his eyebrows with the back of his bare hand. "Of course I'm not really waiting for the doctor."

Meecham's eyes were alert, suspicious. "No?"

"Oh, I'll see him, of course. But what I'm really waiting for— and so are you, if you only knew it—is a destination, a finality, an end of something. My own case is rather special; I'm waiting for an end of fear."

I was right, Meecham thought. *He's a neighborhood nut.* Aloud he said, "You'd better pick a more comfortable place to wait. Move on, now. We don't want any trouble."

The man didn't even hear him. "I've died a thousand times from fear. A thousand deaths, and one would have been enough. A great irony."

"You'd better move on, go home and get some sleep. Have you got a family?"

"A family?" The young man laughed. "I have a great family."

"They may be waiting for you."

"I won't be going home tonight."

"You can't stay here." Meecham glanced briefly at the man's shoes. Like the overcoat, they looked new. He said anyway, "I can let you have a couple of bucks."

"What do you think, that I'm a bum wanting a handout? I'm not a bum."

A car came around the corner, its headlights searched the man's face for a moment like big blind eyes. Meecham recognized him instantly. He had seen him that morning in the county jail, the old-young man with the sensitive face and the swollen dissolute body. The body was hidden now under the tent of his overcoat. His face was bland and unlined, and the falling snow had feathered his eyelashes and made his eyes look dewy and innocent. He was, Meecham thought, about twenty-eight.

He said aloud, "We've met before."

"Yes, I know. I know who you are."

"Oh?"

"You're Mr. Meecham, the girl's lawyer."

Meecham had an abrupt and inexplicable feeling of uneasiness. It was, he thought, like turning around suddenly on a dark night and finding at your heels a silent and vicious dog; nothing is said, nothing is done; the walk continues, the dog behind you, and behind the dog, fear, following you both.

"What's your name?" Meecham said.

"Loftus. Earl Duane Loftus." The young man blinked, and the snow tumbled from his eyelashes down his cheeks in a miniature avalanche. "You'd better go and call the police. You wouldn't mind if I waited inside the house until they arrive? I'm not cold—I never mind the cold—but I'd like to sit down. I tire easily."

"Why should I call the police?"

"I'd like to give them a statement."

"What about?"

"I committed a murder."

"Oh."

"You don't believe me," Loftus said.

"Oh sure, sure I do."

"No. I can tell. First you thought I was a bum, now you think I'm a psycho."

"No, I don't," Meecham lied, without conviction.

"Well, I can't blame you, actually. I guess every murder case attracts a lot of tips and confessions from psychos, people who want punishment or publicity or expiation. I don't fit into any of those classes, Mr. Meecham."

"Of course not," Meecham lied again, wishing that a patrol car would come along, or that the young man would go away quietly, and without a fuss.

"I can see you're still skeptical. You haven't even asked whom I killed."

Meecham felt cold and weary, and a little impatient. "What gave you the idea you killed anyone?"

"The body. The dead body." Loftus' long skinny fingers worked nervously at the lapels of his coat. "I didn't come here following the old lady home. We had a common destination, that's all. I wanted to see the doctor and tell him first. His wife didn't kill Margolis. I did."

Meecham's impatience had grown with his discomfort. "How'd you kill him, with a shotgun as he was going into the post-office to mail a letter?"

Loftus shook his head, very seriously. "No, sir, I didn't. I stabbed him in the neck. Four or five times, I believe."

"Why?"

"I had a good many reasons." He leaned toward Meecham in an almost confidential manner. "I look funny to you, don't I? You think like a lot of people that a man who looks so funny must also be funny in the head. Looks are very important. Very deceiving too. I'm quite sane, quite intelligent even. There's only one thing the matter with me; I am going to die."

"Why are you telling me?"

"You asked why I killed Margolis. Well, that's one of my reasons. Ever since I found out, a year ago, what my chances were, I've been pondering the situation. Since I was going to die anyway, I thought I would take someone with me—rid the world of someone it would be better off without, some incorrigible criminal, perhaps, or a dangerous politician. But when the time and opportunity came, it was Margolis. I wish it could have been someone more important. Margolis was very third-rate."

"He had a wife and two kids."

Loftus' calm was unshaken. "He won't be missed. I've done them a favor."

"Well," Meecham said quietly. "Come inside and sit down."

"Thank you, sir."

They walked, side by side, toward the house. It seemed to Meecham that it was the longest and strangest walk he'd ever taken.

FIVE

Loftus looked at the clock on the mantel. 6:10. So the clock was going, all right, time was passing, but slow and soundless. He missed the noise of ticking. The clock he had in his own room ticked so loud that it often kept him awake. Sometimes in the middle of the night he got up and covered it with a glass bowl that he'd bought in the dime store. The glass smothered the noise a little but didn't obscure the face of the clock.

The room was quiet. Mrs. Hamilton and the blonde girl had gone to another part of the house, and the doctor had come, and, after a long whispered conference in the hall, had gone away again. There were only the four of them left, the two policemen, and Meecham, and Loftus himself.

"Loftus."

Loftus turned. "Yes, sir." He wasn't sure if this was the way to address a sheriff. He had never talked to one before.

"When did you write this?" Cordwink said.

"This afternoon."

"Why?"

"I thought it would be better to write it down myself, to get things very clear. They are, aren't they? Clear?"

Cordwink made a noise in the back of his throat. "Clear as a bell. You thought of everything, Loftus."

"I tried to."

"It makes me wonder whether you might have had a little help with it."

"Who would help me?"

"Well, now. Meecham over here is always willing to lend a hand, especially if…"

"You're off your rocker, Cordwink," Meecham said flatly. "I never saw the man before in my life."

"No?"

"No. And just what do you mean 'help' him with it? You talk as if we're a couple of school kids and I did his homework for him, or something."

Cordwink rustled the papers he held in his hand. There were eight of them, closely written. By moving his head slightly Loftus could see the top sheet. It had been the most difficult to write. He had made so many copies that he knew it by heart: *My name is Earl Duane Loftus. I am writing this without coercion or advice on the part of anyone, and with the full knowledge that it can be used as evidence in a court of law…*

Cordwink was speaking. "This comes at a convenient time for you, Meecham. Your client's in jail, a lot of evidence against her…"

"Circumstantial."

"…and then out of the blue comes a nice pat answer to all your problems."

"But it didn't come out of the blue," Loftus said, blinking his eyes nervously. "Not at all, sir. I intended to admit everything right from the beginning, but I needed some time. I had to do a few things first, personal things. I'm afraid I didn't give much thought to Mrs. Barkeley being held in jail. But then it didn't do her any harm, did it? She's a little spoiled."

"Is she?"

"I think so."

Cordwink's mouth tightened. "There's nothing in what you've written here to indicate that you knew her before last Saturday night."

49

"I didn't know her, not actually. I saw her once, a little over a year ago. I had come to consult Dr. Barkeley, I was feeling so tired and heavy, and I minded the heat so much. I..." He paused, folding his arms to hide his belly. It was my belly that worried me, he thought. It had begun to swell, bigger and bigger. I had nightmares about being a hideous freak, the only man in the world who ever had a baby. It wasn't a baby, but I was a freak, all right. I didn't know it then. I said, it's my nerves, doctor, maybe I need a rest, a change of climate. You need hospital treatment, he said. I went to him three times, and the third time he told me what I had. It was only a word to me then, a pretty word like a girl's name, Leukemia, Leukemia Smith, Leukemia Ann Johnston. Chronic myeloid leukemia, he said. He didn't tell me I was dying. But I knew, I knew. He never sent me a bill.

"Loftus," Cordwink said.

Loftus jerked his head up. "Yes, sir."

"Go on. You were saying?"

"I—oh, yes. Yes. I saw Mrs. Barkeley once when I went to the doctor's office. She was in the yard raking up leaves."

"Did you talk to her?"

"No, oh no. I just passed by."

"Did she notice you?"

"I don't think so."

"Have you ever talked to her?"

"Just on Saturday night, that's the only time."

Cordwink turned to the deputy he had brought with him, a young intense-looking man in a tweed suit. "Dunlop, you're getting all this down?"

"Yes, sir," Dunlop said. "'Just on Saturday night, that's the only time.'"

"When Mrs. Barkeley came into the bar, Loftus, did you recognize her?"

"Of course. She's a very pretty woman."

"What was the name of the bar?"

"It's in there, in my confession."

"Tell me anyway."

"Sam's Café."

"Are you sure? I thought it was Joe's."

Loftus shook his head. "It was Sam's. If you're trying to confuse me, you can't. I remember everything very clearly. I only had one drink, a beer. I was just finishing it when Mrs. Barkeley came up to the bar and sat down beside me. This is all written down, but I suppose you want me to repeat it, just to test me, is that it?"

"Go on."

"She smiled at me and said hello. I was flattered, thinking she might have remembered me. Then I saw how drunk she was, eyes glassy and out of focus, and her smile not real at all, just sort of painted on like a doll's smile."

"What else did she say?"

"You mean her exact words?"

"Yes."

Loftus thought a moment. "She said, 'God, this place stinks.'"

Meecham made a sound like a laugh and covered it with a cough. Cordwink turned and stared at him. "Is something amusing you, Meecham?"

"No." Meecham coughed again. "I have a slight cold."

"Is that a fact? Dunlop."

"Yes, sir," Dunlop said.

"Read that back. Mr. Meecham wants a good laugh."

Dunlop bent over his notes. "'God, this place stinks.'"

"There. Is it as funny as you thought it was, Meecham?"

Meecham looked as if he intended to make a sharp reply but he held it back. "No."

"All right then. What else did Mrs. Barkeley say to you, Loftus?"

"She said she wanted a drink but she'd left her purse in the car. I bought her a beer. She had just started to drink it when Margolis came in. He was an impressive-looking man. I'd seen him before at the county hospital where I go for my X-ray treatments and shots. His firm was building the new T.B. wing and he used to hang around a lot, talking to the nurses. Margolis remembered me too. I'm quite a—freak." He looked down at the floor. "Margolis asked Mrs. Barkeley to leave. She said she didn't want to go home, and why didn't all three of us go to another place for a drink. Margolis humored her. When she started for the door he said I was to come along and he'd give me a lift home. I accepted. I wanted a lift home, but there was more to it than that. I was excited, thrilled as a high-school kid at suddenly becoming a part of all that— glamor, I guess you'd call it. I didn't realize until we got out to the car that offering me a lift home wasn't exactly a noble gesture on Margolis' part. He needed me to help him handle Mrs. Barkeley. She passed out in the back seat. Margolis shook her and swore at her, but she was limp as a rag."

He stopped to wipe the sweat from his face with his handkerchief.

"...and swore at her," Dunlop said in his quick uninterested monotone, "but she was limp as a rag."

Loftus appealed to Cordwink: "I've admitted everything. Why does he have to take all this down?"

"It's routine, for one thing. For another, the statement you're making now will have to be checked with your written confession for discrepancies."

"But I'm guilty, I've..."

"No matter if you write five hundred confessions, you still have to be tried in a court of law to determine the degree of your guilt."

"Yes. Yes, I see now. I didn't realize." I sound so meek, Loftus thought. I don't sound like a murderer at all. Maybe I would be more convincing if I acted belligerent, but I hardly know how.

"Are you ready to continue, Loftus?"

"I—yes, of course. Margolis said he couldn't take Mrs. Barkeley home in that condition, and he asked me if I'd mind helping him get her out to his cottage. It wasn't the first time I'd heard of his cottage. There were rumors around the hospital... I was there so much that I got to know quite a few of the nurses, and that's how I first heard of Margolis and his affairs.

"The cottage was just outside the city limits, on the river. It didn't look like much on the outside, but it was fixed up nice inside—leather furniture and a stone fireplace and some good reproductions hanging on the walls, a Van Gogh, I remember, was one of them."

"Tell me more about the fireplace," Cordwink said.

"Well, there were a pair of fishing rods, crossed, on the wall above it, and on the mantel itself there were several of those big German steins and two hunting knives in leather sheaths."

"Dunlop..." Cordwink made a half-turn. "Was the inside of Margolis' cottage described in any of the papers?"

Dunlop put down his pencil. "A couple of Detroit papers carried a shot of the outside, and the *Tribune*, I think it was, had a shot of the floor where Margolis was found—bloodstains, et cetera."

"No fireplace in the picture?"

"No fireplace."

Loftus smiled anxiously. "I don't read the *Tribune* anyway, sir."

"All right, go on."

"I helped Margolis carry her inside the cottage and put her on the davenport. She was still out cold. Margolis was very angry by this time. I think the two of them must have been quarreling

53

earlier in the evening, and that this was a final straw for Margolis. He began calling her names and shaking her again. It was an ugly scene. I thought of all the things I'd heard about Margolis around the hospital. I thought of—well, it doesn't matter what I thought. I went over to the fireplace. The fire was lit and the room was beginning to get very warm. I picked up one of the hunting knives and took it out of its sheath. Margolis wasn't paying any attention to me. He'd forgotten I was there. I was just a bum, a nobody, a—well, then I did it. I stabbed him in the neck. I'm not very strong and I thought his neck would be the easiest place. It wasn't easy. I had to stab him four or five times. He fell after the first stab, but he didn't die right away. He kept sort of *flopping* around on the floor. The blood was terrible. It got all over me, my gloves and my coat and pants. And the smell—I began to retch. I ran for the door, and I kept on running. I lost my head, forgot about the girl, forgot about everything. All I wanted to do was get away from that blood, that smell. I went home by side streets. I don't know how far I walked, two miles, three miles. No one noticed me particularly. It was late, and it was snowing, big feathery flakes of snow that clung to my clothes and hid the stains. The house was dark when I got home. I let myself into my room and took off the clothes that had blood on them and put them in the back of the wardrobe. That's where they are now."

"In the wardrobe," Cordwink said.

"Yes, 611 Division Street, the left front room. It has its own entrance, that's why the landlady calls it an apartment."

"What did you do on Sunday?"

"I was very weak, I had to stay in bed."

"Didn't see any papers?"

"Not until early Monday morning, that is, this morning. As soon as I read that Mrs. Barkeley was being held, I went down to the jail to see you. You were busy, and I waited in the corridor. Mr. Meecham saw me there."

Meecham nodded. "Yes, I saw him."

"Well, I didn't," Cordwink said. "What happened, Loftus? Lose your nerve?"

"No. I suddenly realized, as I was sitting there, that there were a lot of things I hadn't attended to, and that I'd never get a chance, once I'd confessed. So I walked out again."

"A lot of things you hadn't attended to, such as what?"

"Personal things. I closed my bank account, and sold my car, things like that."

"Listen to this, Loftus." Cordwink turned over the pages until he found what he was looking for. "'I stabbed Margolis deliberately and with intent to kill, and not to protect Mrs. Barkley or myself.' You still claim that?"

"Better think before you answer," Meecham said. "That deliberation and intent business will…"

"Keep out of this, Meecham," Cordwink said, scowling. "You're not his lawyer."

"He needs one."

"He'll get one." Cordwink faced Loftus again. "Have you any money?"

"A little, yes. The past few months I've been able to work. I'm an accountant. That's what my treatments have been for, not so I could live longer, but so I could carry on with my job, live more efficiently."

"How much money? Two thousand? One?"

"Oh, not that much."

"Lawyers come high. The more crooked they are, the bigger their price. That's how they stay out of the booby hatch, by rubbing the lesions on their conscience with greenbacks."

Loftus looked a little puzzled. "Well, if I have to have a lawyer, Mr. Meecham will suit me fine. He's been very kind."

"Kind?" Cordwink raised his eyebrows, exaggeratedly. "This I must hear."

"When he thought I was just a bum, he offered me two dollars."

"Well, well. Where'd you get the two dollars, Meecham, selling phony oil shares to war widows?"

Meecham's smile was a little strained. "I object to the question on the grounds that it is intimidating and forms a conclusion."

Dunlop put down his pencil, and said, with a faint whine, "When everybody keeps talking like this, I don't know what to write down. Everybody shouldn't keep talking like this."

"Don't write anything," Cordwink said. "Call a patrol car and take Loftus down and book him."

I'm going to jail, Loftus thought. But he still couldn't quite believe it. Jail was for criminals, for thieves and thugs, for brutal angry lawless men. He said, with the surprise and disbelief evident in his voice: "I'm going to—to jail?"

"For the present, yes."

"Why do you say, for the present?"

"We have no facilities at the jail for looking after a dy——a sick man. There's a prison ward at the County Hospital. You'll be transferred there eventually."

"The County Hospital." Loftus laughed, holding his hands over his belly. It hurt him to laugh, but he couldn't help it. "That's funny, isn't it? The final irony. After all that's happened, I'll end up where I started—in a ward at the County Hospital."

The sound of his laughter faded, though his mouth kept grinning. He saw Cordwink and Meecham exchange uneasy glances. "You're uncomfortable, aren't you?—disturbed?—you wish you'd never seen me? Yes, it's the same everywhere I go, I make people uncomfortable. I don't have any friends. No one wants to be near me, people are afraid to be near a man who's walking a step ahead of death. I make them too conscious of their own fate, and they hate me for it. I'm not blaming them, no, I understand how they feel. I loathe myself more than anyone could loathe me. I loathe this decaying body that I'm trapped inside, hopelessly trapped inside. This isn't me, this grotesque body, it is my prison. What prison have you to offer that could be half so terrible?"

He didn't realize that he was crying until he felt the sting of salt on his lips. He sometimes cried when he was alone at night and the hours seemed so ironically endless; but never in front of anyone, not even his wife on the day she left him. He wiped his eyes with his coat sleeve, ashamed that he had broken down in front of these three men.

Cordwink stared out of the window, motionless, his face like granite. Inside, he felt something begin to move, like a steel claw, reaching out and clutching his stomach, squeezing. *It could be me. Or Alma and the kids. Don't let it happen. Me or Alma and the kids.*

A pair of headlights swerved up the driveway. He glanced across the room at Loftus. Loftus had slumped forward in his chair, his hands covering his eyes. The back of his neck looked very young, a boy's neck, thin and vulnerable and white as wax.

"Loftus."

There was no reply, no stirring in response to his name.

"Loftus," Cordwink said again. "The car is here."

Loftus raised his head slowly. He seemed dazed, as if he'd flown his prison, had gone miles and years away, and was now returning, like a soul to hell.

"I'm ready," Loftus said.

SIX

611 Division Street was a three-story red-brick house on the out-skirts of the college district. Light and noise poured from nearly every window. On the second floor two young men were bending over a microscope. In the adjoining room a boy sat at a table by the window, absorbed in the blare of the radio beside him, his head resting on an open book. Meecham couldn't see into any of the rooms on the top floor, but it sounded as if a party was going on up there. There was a continuous babble of voices punctuated by sudden peals of laughter.

The left part of the lower floor was dark and the shades were drawn.

Following Cordwink up the sidewalk Meecham thought, it's a funny place for Loftus to live—a dying man in the midst of all this noise and youth.

The sidewalk forked to the left. A little path no more than a foot wide had been shoveled through the snow and sprinkled with cinders. This was Loftus' private entrance.

Cordwink took out the ring of keys that Loftus had given him. "Still want to tag along, Meecham?"

"Certainly."

"What do you expect me to find?"

"The bloodstained clothes he was wearing Saturday night."

"You seem to have a lot of confidence in that confession. Wishful thinking, Meecham?"

"Could be."

"You and Loftus are kind of palsy for a couple of guys who never met before."

"I'm palsy with everyone."

"Yeah. You got a heart of gold, haven't you? Cold and yellow."

"You're getting to be a sour old character if I ever saw one."

Cordwink inserted one of the keys into the lock. It didn't fit, but the second one did. The flimsy door, curtained at the top, swung inward. "By the way, it wouldn't be quite ethical to take on a second client while your first client is still in jail."

"She won't be in jail long. Your forty-eight hours are nearly up, Cordwink. By tomorrow morning you have to charge her or release her."

"And if she's released, you'd take on a lost cause like Loftus?"

"One minute you're implying that his confession is a phony and the next minute he's a lost cause. Make up your mind."

"He's a lost cause to you, anyway. He hasn't much money."

"Well?"

"Or at least that's what he claims." Cordwink turned on the light switch inside the door, but he didn't look at the room. He was watching Meecham. "Suppose you were in Loftus' shoes and wanted some money."

"Money isn't much good, where's he's going."

"Suppose he didn't want it for himself. For a relative, maybe, or a close friend. It seems to me that Loftus had something very valuable to sell—his absolutely certain knowledge that he's going to die anyway. No matter what he does, he has nothing to lose."

"So?"

"So he committed a murder. For money."

"Whose money?"

"Virginia Barkeley's."

"That sounds reasonable enough," Meecham said calmly, "except for a few little things. First, Mrs. Barkeley only met Loftus once, in a bar, for about five minutes. That's not quite long enough to arrange a big deal like murder."

"She could have known him before. They'd both deny that, naturally, if there's a deal on."

"In the second place, if she paid him to kill Margolis, she wouldn't have arranged the matter so that she'd be caught as she was."

"Maybe she's very, very subtle."

"In the third place she hasn't any money and neither has her husband. I've checked. They live up to their income, the house is mortgaged and the furniture isn't paid for."

"There are ways of raising money."

"And in the fourth place you don't even know that Loftus has any money."

"I'll find out."

"Your trouble is stubbornness, Cordwink. You were sure Mrs. Barkeley was guilty and you can't admit you were wrong even with Loftus' confession staring you in the face."

"What's staring me in the face is a lot of funny coincidences and right in the middle of them is a lawyer called Meecham."

"Is that a fact?"

"That's one. Another one has just occurred to me. Suppose Loftus was paid for services rendered, what did he do with the money?"

Meecham said wearily, "He dug a hole in the back yard and buried it."

"I figure he gave it to someone, either the party he wanted it for in the first place, or a go-between."

"Me?"

"You."

"Whom am I going between, or between whom am I going? Oh, hell. You know I never saw Loftus until today."

60

"That's your story."

"His, too."

"It would be, of course, if the two of you are working in collusion."

Meecham lit a cigarette. There was no ash tray in the room that he could see, so he put the burnt match in his pocket. "So now you've dreamed up a place for the money you've dreamed up. Want to see my wallet? Check books? Or maybe I'm wearing a money belt. Why don't you check?"

"Don't worry, I will. When the time comes."

"You can waste a lot of time chasing little bright butterflies, Cordwink."

"I like the exercise."

Meecham raised his head. He saw that the Sheriff was looking rather pleased with himself, and he wondered whether Cordwink really believed in his own theory or whether he was merely needling him. Cordwink hated all lawyers, but his hatred wasn't a personal one. It was a matter of principle: he hated lawyers because he believed their sole objective was to circumvent the law.

Cordwink began to circle the room, his eyes moving from object to object with alert precision.

The room was fairly large, and fitted out for light housekeeping. In one corner, half-hidden by a painted cardboard screen, was a small sink and a two-burner gas plate and a table. The bed was a studio couch neatly covered with a blue and yellow chenille spread, and above it, high on the wall, a trio of college pennants was nailed:

Illinois. Arbana. Yale.

The pennants were very old and very dusty. They probably didn't belong to Loftus, Meecham thought. They had been on the wall when he moved in and he left them there because they were too high to reach. Anyway, there they were, emphasizing the transient feeling of the room, symbols of college boys who were no longer boys, football teams that were forgotten, textbooks left to mildew, with silverfish camping, sleek and comfortable, between the pages.

A room for transients, with Loftus the last, the most transient of them all. It was as if Loftus had known this and had taken pains to obliterate his traces. The whole room, except for the pennants, was scrupulously clean. There were no clothes or shoes lying around, the top of the bureau held only an alarm clock with a glass bowl inverted over it, and the wastebasket beside the desk was empty. Whatever had been in the wastebasket—letters, bills, check stubs, pages from a diary?—they were all gone now. There was no clue to Loftus' mind and personality in the room except for the books that filled the high narrow bookcase.

The books were oddly assorted: a few novels, two anthologies of poetry, *How to Win at Canasta*, a biography of Pasteur and a Bible—but most of them concerned psychology and medicine. Cecil's *Textbook of Medicine*, *Cancer and Its Causes*, *The Neurotic Personality of Our Time*, *Peace of Mind*, *Release from Fear*, *Alcoholism and Its Causes*, *The Alcoholic and Allergy*, *A New View of Alcoholism*, *How to Treat the Alcoholic*, *Drinking Problems*, *Glandular Deficiency in Alcoholism*.

Cordwink, too, was staring at the books. "He doesn't look like a lush," he said finally.

"No."

"You can't always tell, though. One of the worst lushes I ever knew used to take up collection in the Methodist church. No one even knew he took a drink until one night he started hopping around the house trying to get out of the way of the fish. He thought there were little fish flopping all over the floor. Bats and snakes and beetles I'd heard of, but never little fish. It was creepy, made the bottom of my feet kind of ticklish. Funny, eh?"

"What happened to him?"

"He hit the real skids after that. Landed in jail four or five times that year for non-support, disturbing, petty theft. He always had a whale of an excuse. Drunks are the wildest liars in the world."

"Loftus isn't a drunk."

"Maybe not."

There was no closet in the room, but between the studio couch and the screen that hid the gas plate, a seven-foot walnut wardrobe stood against the wall. It was a massive piece of furniture, with a big old-fashioned plain lock. There was no key to fit it on the keyring Loftus had given him, so Cordwink forced the lock with the small blade of his jacknife. When the door opened, the pungent smell of moth crystals filled the room. Cordwink sneezed, and sneezed again.

There was hardly enough clothing inside the wardrobe to justify the lavish use of moth crystals: two suits, well-worn but cleaned and pressed, a sweater, shoes, a pair of galoshes, a khaki baseball cap, some pajamas; and on the floor, three suitcases. Two of them were empty. The third Cordwink took out and placed on the studio couch.

Pasted across the top of the suitcase was a faded Railway Express consignment slip: From Mrs. Charles E. Loftus, 231 Oak Street, Kincaid, Michigan, to Mr. Earl Duane Loftus, 611 Division Street, Arbana, Michigan. Value of contents, $50.00

"His mother," Cordwink said. "Or maybe his sister-in-law. Or maybe it doesn't even matter."

The value of the original contents might have been fifty dollars. The present contents had little monetary value: an old trench coat, a blue serge suit, and a pair of brown oxfords, all of them stained with blood.

Cordwink pressed down the lid of the suitcase. "I'd like to talk to the woman who runs this place. Loftus said she's a Mrs. Hearst. Go and get her, will you?"

"Why don't you? You have the authority."

"This stuff is evidence. I wouldn't trust you alone with it."

Meecham colored. "What the hell do you think I'd do, grab it and take off for South America?"

"I don't know and I'm not going to find out. Be a good boy now, Meecham, and co-operate, and some day you may be District Attorney, then you can kick me in the teeth if I've got any teeth left by that time."

"Who are you kidding? You haven't got any left now."

Cordwink's eyes narrowed, but he didn't make any reply. He crossed the room to the door that led into the hallway of the house, unlocked it, and motioned Meecham out with a curt nod.

Meecham went out, quite meekly. He felt a little ashamed of himself for making the crack about Cordwink's teeth. Nearly everyone in town knew that Cordwink had had his front teeth knocked out in a fight with two berserk sailors who were equipped with brass knuckles. The sailors went to a military prison, Cordwink went to the dentist, and the brass knuckles went into his pile of impounded weapons that included everything from sawed-off shotguns to paring knives.

Meecham followed the hall past an immense high-ceilinged dining room into the kitchen. It was a big old-fashioned kitchen, designed not merely for cooking and eating, but for all kinds of family living. There was a card table with a plastic canasta set, a rocking chair, a record player, a bookcase and a couch with a blanket neatly folded at the foot. A woman stood at the sink, wiping dishes and humming to herself.

Her voice and figure were youthful, and her light hair was cut girlishly short and curled close to her head. But when she turned, hearing Meecham approach, he saw that she was about forty. Her hair was gray, not blonde as it appeared at first, and the skin around her sharp blue eyes was creased and dry, like crepe paper.

She smiled at Meecham as she rolled down the sleeves of her dress and buttoned them at the wrists. Her smile was not artificial exactly, but facile, as if she was accustomed to smiling in all kinds of situations and at all kinds of people. "Were you looking for someone?"

"Yes, the owner of the house."

"The bank owns it," she said crisply. "Arbana Trust and Savings. I rent it."

"You're Mrs. Hearst?"

"Yes."

"I'm Eric Meecham. I'm a friend of Mr. Loftus."

"A friend of Earl's? Isn't that *nice*, it really *is*." Out of habit, she spoke with a little too much emphasis. It made her enthusiasm, which was real, sound forced. "For a minute there I thought you were going to try and sell me something. *Not* that I wouldn't like to buy something, but nobody ever got rich on college boys. They're nice boys, all of them, boys from *good* homes. But what with taxes the way..." She paused, suddenly frowning. "You're from out of town?"

"No, I live here."

"I just wondered. Earl's never mentioned you. He hasn't many friends and he usually tells me things. I—is anything the matter? Where is Earl? Where *is* he?"

"I can't say, definitely."

"I knew something was up. He always has supper with me Monday nights. Tonight he didn't come, didn't phone. I waited an hour. Everything was ruined. Where is he?"

"In jail."

"In *jail*? Why, that's crazy. Why, Earl is one of the quietest, most *refined*…"

"The Sheriff is in his room now. He wants to talk to you."

"To me? A sheriff? Why I—I don't know what to say. This isn't some kind of trick one of my boys put you up to? They play tricks on me sometimes, not meaning to be cruel."

"There's no trick," Meecham said. "I'm a long way from college."

"A sheriff," she repeated, in a strained voice. "I'll talk to him, if I must. But I've nothing to say. Nothing. Earl is a perfect gentleman. And more than that, too. You only see him now, when he's sick." She hesitated, as if she would have liked to say more about Loftus, but decided this was not the time or place. "All right, I'll talk to him. Some mistake has been made somewhere, of that I'm sure."

She preceded Meecham down the hall, wiping her hands nervously on her apron and casting uneasy glances up the staircase to her left, obviously afraid that one of the "boys from good homes" would come down and see her talking to a policeman.

Meecham followed her into Loftus' room and closed the door. "Mrs. Hearst, this is the Sheriff, Mr. Cordwink."

Cordwink acknowledged the introduction with a brief nod. "Sit down, Mrs. Hearst. I just want to check up on a few things about Earl Loftus."

The woman didn't sit down. She didn't even advance into the room, but stood rigidly with her back against the wall, her hands clenched in the pockets of her apron. "I don't understand why you're here. Earl hasn't—*done* anything?"

"That's what I'm trying to find out," Cordwink said. "How long has he been with you?"

"Lived here? A year, almost a year."

"You know him pretty well, then?"

"I—yes. We are friends."

"He confides in you?"

"Yes, you understand, I'm not like a *mother* to him, the way I am to some of my boys. No indeed, Earl's different, more mature. Our conversations are very stimulating. Why, he talks as mature as any man my—my own age."

"I notice that he has his own telephone and mailbox."

"Yes, this little apartment is completely separate from the rest of the house."

"Then you wouldn't, naturally, be able to keep as close track of him as you would of your regular roomers."

Mrs. Hearst's mouth looked pinched. "I don't have to keep *track* of anyone."

"What I meant was…"

"I know what you meant. You meant, do I snoop in on other people's telephone conversations and examine their mail. No, I don't. And in Earl's case it wouldn't even be necessary. He tells me everything."

There was a brief silence before Cordwink spoke again, in a quiet, amiable voice: "He seems, on the surface, to be quite an exceptional young man."

"Not just on the surface. He's exceptional all through. Very intelligent, Earl is, and very polite and considerate, doesn't drink or smoke or run around with women."

"He's married, isn't he?"

"Married? Why, of course not. He would certainly have told me, and he's never mentioned a wife. Just his mother. He's devoted to his mother. She lives out of town, but she came to see him last summer. A very refined type of woman. She's ill most of the time, that's why she doesn't come to see him oftener. Earl himself isn't very—very well."

"Yes, I know that." Cordwink went over to the studio couch and lifted the lid of the suitcase. "I suppose you're familiar with Loftus' clothes?"

"His clothes? That's a funny question. I don't understand."

Cordwink picked up the wrinkled bloodstained trench coat, quite naturally and casually, as if it was an ordinary piece of clothing. There was no indication, in his movements or expression, of his extreme distaste for the sight of blood, the feelings it gave him, of loss, futility, vulnerability. The blood on this worn and dirty coat had been the end of a man and might be the end of another.

He said calmly, "Do you, for instance, recognize this coat, Mrs. Hearst?"

"I—don't know. It's so wrinkled. I can't... What are those marks?"

"Blood."

She drew in her breath suddenly, gaspingly, like an exhausted swimmer. "I don't like this. I don't like it, I say. Where's Earl? Where *is* he? You've got no right prying into his things like this! How do I know you're policemen? How do I know you're not a pair...?"

"Here's my identification." Cordwink took his badge out of his pocket and showed it to her. "Mr. Meecham isn't a policeman, he's a lawyer. As for prying into Loftus' things, I'm doing it with his consent. Here are his own keys. He gave them to me."

The woman sat down, suddenly and heavily. "What—what did Earl do?"

"He says he killed a man."

She stared, round-eyed, glassy-eyed, into the corner of the room. "Here? *Here* in this house?"

"No."

"Earl didn't—couldn't—it's impossible."

"He says he did."

"But you can't believe him. I've often thought, time and time again I've thought, that someday that terrible disease would affect his mind, would…"

"His mind seems clear enough," Cordwink said.

"But you don't *know* Earl. He could never harm anyone. He hated to kill anything. Why—why, once there was a mouse in his room—last fall—I wanted to set a trap but he wouldn't let me. He said the mouse was so tiny and harmless…"

"Mrs. Hearst."

"I'm *telling* you, Earl *wouldn't*."

"This is his coat, isn't it?"

She turned her head away and stared at the wall. "Yes."

"And this suit? The shoes? Please look at them, Mrs. Hearst. You can't identify something without looking at it."

She glanced briefly at the suit and shoes and then away again. "They're Earl's."

"No question about it?"

"I said they're Earl's. Now can I go? I've had a great shock, a terrible shock."

"In a minute," Cordwink said. "The trench coat, and the serge suit—were these the clothes Loftus usually wore when he was going out in the evening, say?"

"Why?" she said bitterly. "Don't you think they were good enough to go out in? Well, maybe they weren't! But they were the only ones he had. He couldn't afford any more."

"When I saw him an hour ago he was wearing a new topcoat, new suit, new shoes. All of them looked expensive."

"I don't care! I don't know what you're implying, and I don't *care*!"

"Did you ever lend him money, Mrs. Hearst?"

"I—no! Never! He'd never have taken it, never have borrowed money from a woman, never!"

"All right," Cordwink said. Privately he wondered how much, and when. "Then you didn't lend him any money, say, this morning?"

"No!"

"Did you see him this morning?"

"Yes."

"When?"

"When I was shoveling off the walk, about seven-thirty."

"What exactly did you say to him?"

"I said—I said, 'Earl you can't go like that, in just a sweater and slacks, it's winter, you'll catch cold.'"

"And he said?"

"That he'd sent his coat to the cleaner's and that anyway he wasn't cold. I asked him where he was off to, so early. And he said he was going downtown to see about selling his car. He said it wasn't working so well, it was just a nuisance in the winter, so he thought he'd sell it, and then, in the spring, maybe he'd—he'd be feeling better and could work more and buy a—a new car. I said, just joking, how about a Cadillac, then you can take me for a ride. And he said there—wasn't anyone he'd rather take for a ride in a Cadillac than—than me."

She looked toward the window as if she was trying to see, not the dark of a winter night, but a morning in spring, with Earl well again and at the wheel of his new car.

"As you know now," Cordwink said, "he didn't send his coat to the cleaner's. It was here all the time, locked inside the wardrobe.

He had approximately forty hours to dispose of it, but he apparently made no attempt to. That's curious, don't you think, Mrs. Hearst?"

"Curious," she repeated dully. "Yes. It's curious. Everything's curious."

"Do you clean Loftus' roo——apartment?"

"Go on, *call* it a room. It's not an apartment, it's just a room. I know it's just a room, and Earl knows it and everyone…" She stopped, holding the back of her hand to her mouth. "I clean it twice a week, Tuesday and Saturday. I don't have to do it, it's not included in his rent. I do it for—because I like to," she added defiantly. "I *like* to clean."

"Take another look around now, Mrs. Hearst. Is this the way his room usually looked?"

"No."

"What's different about it?"

"A lot of his things are gone."

"Clothes?"

"Not clothes. Personal little things, like his desk set, for instance. He had a very nice desk set, onyx, quite expensive. His mother gave it to him. His mother's picture is gone too, it was in a silver frame. And his radio—he used to keep his radio on the table over there."

"Have you any idea what happened to the missing objects?"

"They could have been—s-stolen." But she stumbled over the answer. It was fairly obvious, both to Meecham and to Cordwink, that she didn't believe the articles had been stolen.

"Or pawned, maybe," Cordwink said. "Was he in the habit of pawning things?"

"He—when he *had* to, when he was desperate. He had such terrible expenses. And then there's his mother, he sends her money.

Last fall he scrimped and saved to send her some and when he did she blew it all in—went out and bought the desk set I told you about, and mailed it to him. It was a nice gesture, of course, only it was such a *foolish* thing to do. But then, she's very refined, she doesn't realize that people have to scrounge around for money these days."

"You think, then, that Loftus pawned this stuff of his that's missing?"

"Yes."

"Any idea where?"

"There's a little place in the east end, right next to the bowling alley. Devine's, it's called."

"Did Loftus tell you that's where he usually went?"

"I—no. No, he didn't." Her skin looked flushed. "I found a pawn ticket once when I was dusting his bureau. It was for his wrist watch. He never got the watch back. He told me he'd lost it. It wasn't a real lie, Earl never lies. It was just a fib to save his pride. Being poor," she said, "having to pawn things, that's nothing to be ashamed of. But Earl isn't used to it the way some people are. His father was well-to-do—he was a broker in Detroit before he died—and of course when Earl was working steadily he got a very good salary. Being poor is new to Earl. It's his disease that's dragged him down, his disease and his mom——No. No, I won't say that. His mother can't help herself, she's very refined."

Cordwink lit a cigarette. He rarely smoked, and the package from which he had taken the cigarette looked as though it had been in his pocket for months. He said, "When did you last see Loftus wearing this trench coat?"

"Saturday night. I was on my way to the hockey game, one of my boys is on the team. I met Earl on the sidewalk out in front of the house. I stopped to chat, I always do, and Earl said he'd just finished dinner downtown and that he was going to bed early because he was tired."

"After the game you got home around...?"

"Eleven, it was just about eleven. Earl had gone to bed by that time."

"Are you sure of that?"

"Well, I *thought* he'd gone to bed. It never occurred to me that he hadn't, and his lights were off."

"Did you see him on Sunday at all?"

"No, Sunday's my day off. I always go over to Chelsea to visit my sister and her kids. My sister and I had a little disagreement, nothing serious, but I left earlier than usual. I got home around 8:30. Earl's light was on, I saw it shining under the door when I went into the hall. I thought of dropping in on him a minute, I was upset and Earl always cheers me up. But when I stopped outside his door he was talking on the telephone so I went on up to my room."

"How long did you pause there, in the hall?"

"Oh, half a minute, no longer."

"And you heard him talking?"

"Yes."

"But not necessarily on the phone."

"I—no, not necessarily, but..."

"In fact, there may have been someone in here with him."

"Well, I can't swear to it, of course, but I'm sure there wasn't anyone here. Earl never has company."

"No girl friends?"

Mrs. Hearst frowned. "No, *none*. Of that I *am* sure. He doesn't bother with girls, young girls."

"Was it a question of money?"

"No. Earl considers himself—well, deformed. He told me once that he couldn't expect any woman to go out with a freak like he

73

was." She rubbed her eyes with the corner of her apron. "He isn't a freak. It hurt me, his saying that. He *isn't* a freak. A lot of women would be glad to—to look after him, see that he got the proper rest and food and didn't go traipsing around in the cold without his galoshes and overcoat. A lot of women would be—would be…"

She hid her face in her apron, in silent grief. Watching her, Meecham wondered if the grief was for Loftus, or for all the women like herself who wanted a man to look after.

His eyes shifted to Cordwink. Cordwink's face was grim and the cigarette he was smoking was chewed at one end like a cigar. He opened his mouth, and Meecham thought he was going to say something to the woman. But the Sheriff didn't speak. Instead, he went over and helped Mrs. Hearst out of the chair and guided her out into the hallway as if she were blind.

When he came back he slammed the door shut behind him and looked bitterly across the room at Meecham. "Okay, you got any smart cracks to make, Meecham?"

"No."

"That's good, because I'm not in the mood to listen to any." He closed the suitcase with a bang, picked it up and turned off the lights. "I'll drop you off at Barkeley's so you can pick up your car."

"Thanks."

Cordwink didn't speak again until he got into his car and pulled away from the curb.

"The fact is," he said, "I'm a very emotional man where women are concerned."

74

SEVEN

The light of morning coming in through the barred window was dingy, and along the corridor a cool damp wind blew, erratically, first one way and then the other.

Miss Jennings wore a heavy cardigan over her brown dress, and instead of piling her hair high on top of her head as usual, this morning she had let it hang to keep the draft off her neck. As Miss Jennings was in the habit of pointing out, to anyone who was interested and a great many who weren't, weather never bothered her, she rose above it. The clicking of her heels against the floor was overpoweringly cheerful, and she was humming, off-beat and off-key, but with a good deal of spirit.

Virginia pretended not to hear either the footsteps or the humming. She ignored Miss Jennings right up to the last moment; and then it was no longer possible to ignore her because Miss Jennings took her keyring and slid it playfully and noisily across the bars of the cell like a child running a stick along an iron fence.

"Hi!" Miss Jennings always addressed her charges in a good loud voice, as if out of a conviction that imprisonment, like age, impaired the hearing. "Well, you're all prettied up already. That's good, because someone wants to see you right away."

"If it's that greasy little psychiatrist again tell him to go peddle his dreams."

"Now, really. Now, is that any way to talk about nice Dr. Maguire? Besides it's not him—he. It's Mr. Meecham. He has a big surprise for you."

"I wonder."

"He has, too. Guess what it is."

"I don't like guessing games."

"Oh, don't be a little old spoilsport. Go on, guess."

"I'm going home," Virginia said.

"Yes! How about that now, aren't you happy? Aren't you surprised?"

"My mother sent me a message last night. So did Meecham."

"Oh. Well, they couldn't have known for *sure*, though. The lab reports weren't in, the blood, and so forth."

"What blood?"

"Why, he had blood all over his clothes, same as you had. They say he's a nice young man, no record or anything. What amazes me is the amount of blood in a person, it's simply amazing."

"I'd rather not talk about it."

"Well, all right," Miss Jennings smiled, rising above the blood as she rose above the weather.

She unlocked the cell door and Virginia stepped out into the corridor. She was pale, and the skin around her eyes looked blue, as if bruised by pressing thumbs.

"My, my," Miss Jennings said. "You don't look one bit happy. 'Fess up now, you're sorry to be leaving us."

"Oh, sure."

"You've been treated well, haven't you?"

"Great. Just great. I'll recommend the place to all my friends."

Miss Jennings was still wearing her smile but it sagged in places like a worn-out dress. "You're a sarcastic little snip, aren't you?"

"So?"

"You think you're so goddam smart all the time. All the time making smart talk. Oh, I heard your remarks about me to Mr. Meecham yesterday."

"I knew you were too good to be true, Jennings."

There was a thin line of white around the edges of Miss Jennings' mouth. "I know you and your type. Jeering all the time, jeering at decent hardworking respectable people. I hate you. You hear that? I just hate you!"

"Oh, can it," Virginia said. "Who cares?"

"And I'm sorry you're leaving. I hope you'll be back, next time for keeps." She unlocked the door into the main corridor and the keys on the big keyring clanked viciously. "You can go from here by yourself."

"Thanks."

"The girls that come in here and go out again, I always try to give them a nice send-off. But you, I wouldn't even say goodbye to you. I think you're a cold, bad, nasty woman and to hell with you."

She shut the door between them with a decisive bang. All the way down the corridor Virginia could hear the clanking of metal against metal. It sounded as though Miss Jennings was slamming her keys against a wall in time to some rhythm of rage in her heart.

I'm not, Virginia thought, *I'm not a cold nasty woman.*

The door of the Sheriff's office was open, and Meecham was waiting for her inside, with a briefcase under his arm. Cordwink was there too, hunched over a desk that was strewn with papers. On a bench along the wall sat a white-faced young man in a gray prison uniform. The young man was staring at Virginia with a curious kind of intensity. She had an uneasy feeling that there was some silent communication in that glance, that he was trying to say something to her, or ask her something.

No introductions were made, no greetings exchanged. Not a word was spoken until Cordwink said, in his low heavy voice, "Do you recognize this man, Mrs. Barkeley?"

"Not by name. I think I've seen him before, though."

"Where?"

"I don't remember. Anywhere—on the street or at Paul's office or in a bar. I get around quite a few places."

"It was in a bar," Loftus said, very quickly. "Sam's—Saturday night, you talked to me..."

"Keep out of this, Loftus."

Cordwink slapped the desk to emphasize the order. Loftus blinked nervously, but he went right on talking: "I'm only trying to help, Mr. Cordwink. What difference does it make if she remembers me? I've admitted fifty times that I killed Margolis. All these questions and interviews and tests—they aren't going to change anything." He turned to Virginia. "I asked Mr. Meecham to tell you but now I can tell you myself. I'm sorry about your having to stay in jail for a couple of days like this."

"That's—all right." Under the glaring ceiling lights her face was as white as Loftus', and the half-circles under her eyes made her look old and tired and hard. She whirled suddenly and faced Meecham. "I—couldn't we get out of here? I want to get *out* of here."

"All right," Meecham said. "That suit you, Cordwink?"

"It has to." Cordwink stood up. "The papers are all signed, nothing's stopping you, the door's open, go on."

"What about your suitcase, Virginia?"

"To hell with the suitcase," Virginia said harshly. "I just want to get out of here."

Her departure was as wordless as her entrance. No one said goodbye, see you again, glad to have met you. Virginia walked out of the door and down the corridor so rapidly that Meecham had to hurry to catch up with her. Even when she reached the main door she didn't stop to put on her coat. She just held it around her shoulders as she went out, and the arms of the coat flopped back and forth in the rising wind, making silly boneless little gestures.

The sidewalk was dirty with slush and on the road the cars swished by with splatters of mud. Even the wind was dirty. Somewhere, in the north of Canada, it had started out fresh, but it had picked up dirt on its journey, smoke and dust and particles of soot.

They stood in silence, side by side, at the intersection until the light turned green. Then they crossed the road to the parking lot where Meecham had left his car.

The car was locked. With only a slight hesitation Meecham unlocked his own door first and got in the car. Then he leaned across the seat and unlocked the other door for Virginia. The little amenities of politeness seemed as inappropriate and futile here as they had in the Sheriff's office.

Meecham laid his brief case on the seat between them and started the car and switched on the heater. A cold blast of air gushed noisily from the heater.

Virginia reached over and turned the heater off again. "It makes too much noise."

"All right."

"Well, I did what you told me to. Didn't I?"

"More or less."

"I said that he looked familiar, that I'd seen him before. Isn't that what you meant in the note you sent me last night?"

Meecham nodded.

"It's not true though. I've never seen him before, not in Sam's or any other bar or any other place."

"You had quite a few memory lapses on Saturday night."

"I remember talking to someone at Sam's but it wasn't this man. I'd have remembered him because he looks like Willett before Willett began to get fat."

"Willett?"

79

"My older brother. When you meet someone who looks like your own brother, you don't forget him, do you?"

"I haven't got a brother."

"You know what I mean. Don't be so damned annoying, Meecham."

"*Me*, annoying." He turned left at the next intersection. The driver of the car behind him began to sound his horn furiously.

"You didn't make a signal," Virginia said. "If conversation interferes with your driving..."

"Your conversation interferes with my thinking," Meecham said acidly. "You forget some things, you remember some things. The things you're supposed to remember you forget, and the things you're supposed to forget you remember."

"I can't help that."

"Look, you just got out of jail ten minutes ago. Do you want to talk yourself right back in?"

"I thought you were my lawyer. Aren't you supposed to be able to tell everything to your lawyer?"

"Theoretically, yes. But let's get one point straight. What you told me just now—and very positively—was that you never saw Loftus before in your life. You may believe that, but I don't. The evidence is against it. The fact that you'd been drinking heavily all evening makes your memory unreliable anyway. Then there's Loftus' own statement, and his report of some of your remarks to him. Loftus claims that you said among other things, God, this place stinks. One of the bartenders at Sam's overheard it, and identified you as the woman who said it. He has a half-interest in the place, and I think you hurt his feelings. Well, are you still sure you never saw Loftus in your life until this morning?"

"I'm positive."

"I know one definition of positive—being wrong at the top of your voice."

"All right, I may be wrong." She sounded depressed, listless. "It doesn't matter much anyway, does it? When is Claude going to be buried?"

"This afternoon." It was the first time he had heard her use Margolis' first name or indicate in any way that she had been interested in him.

"I wouldn't go to his funeral even if I could. I hate dead people." She huddled, shivering, inside the big plaid coat. "I remember once when I was at school, the mother of one of my friends died, and I went home with the girl to cheer her up. Her mother was at the undertaker's, they hadn't quite finished—fixing her up. The girl combed her mother's hair and fixed her glasses. The damned glasses kept slipping down that dead face, the girl kept putting them in place again. It was ghastly; I almost screamed. Do you have a cigarette?"

"Here."

"Thanks. Shall I light one for you, too?"

"All right."

She lit two cigarettes and gave him one. "Tell me, Meecham, are you on the level?"

"Ask a stupid question and you get a stupid answer. Sure, I am."

"I don't think it's so stupid. You must get lots of opportunities and meet lots of funny people."

"I do, indeed," Meecham said dryly.

"Speaking of mothers, how much is my mother paying you?"

"For what?"

"She *is* paying you?"

"She offered to. I haven't sent her a bill."

"How much are you going to bill her for?"

"I haven't thought about it."

"Well, think now. How much?"

"What is this anyway?" Meecham said, turning his head briefly to look at her. "What's up?"

"She owns quite a bit of real estate back home. Two apartment houses in Pasadena and one in Westwood, and so on."

"Why tell me?"

"So that you'd know she could afford to pay—oh, quite a lot."

"I'm supposed to bill her for quite a lot, eh?"

"She can afford it, I tell you."

"Then when Christmas comes around in a couple of weeks I send you a nice little present, is that it?"

"Sort of."

"It sounds nasty," Meecham said. "And you sound nasty."

"It sounds worse than it is. I like my mother. I'm not trying to chisel her on anything. I can get money from her any time, only I hate to ask her. She always has to know why and what for. This way it would be the same money actually, only I wouldn't have to answer any questions."

"It still sounds nasty. What do you want the money for?"

"Questions, questions. Nobody trusts me."

"What do you want the money for?"

"To run away," she said earnestly.

"Where to?"

"It wouldn't be running away if I told you where. Besides, I haven't decided, and it doesn't matter where as long as it's far away and the climate's good."

He glanced at her again. Her listlessness had gone, and she looked very sincere and hopeful about her new project of running away. But it was a childish hopefulness, without a plan behind it or a foundation under it. "Away" would be pleasant simply because it wasn't "here."

"It will be good for me, good for my morale, to get away," Virginia said. "Carney thinks I'm bad, and Paul thinks I'm a fool. They're both very good people, virtuous people. But it's hard to live with anyone who sets up standards you can't ever reach." She paused to draw on her cigarette. "And now this. This business about Claude. I'll never live it down. No one will ever believe that I wasn't one of Claude's *women*. You don't believe it, Meecham. Do you?"

"I could."

"I wasn't, anyway. I went out with him a few times because he was a wonderful dancer."

It wasn't very convincing, in view of the evidence of the quarrel the two of them had had on Saturday night. But Meecham didn't say anything.

They had come to a railroad crossing just as the signal turned red and the crossing barriers were being lowered into place. A freight train began to move very slowly down the track, heading west. Virginia strained forward in her seat and watched it intensely, watched each car roll ponderously past as if she was wishing she was on one of them, heading west to some place where the climate was good.

He felt sorry for her. The feeling disturbed him, so he turned his attention to the printing on the sides of the freight cars. Michigan Central. Rock Island. Burlington. Atchison, Topeka and Santa Fe. Union Pacific. Grand Rapids. C.P.R. Do Not Hump. And, in chalk, on the bulging belly of a tank car, KILROY WAS HERE, followed by a spirited reply, WHO WASN'T, JOE AND HOWIE.

A hundred cars—oil and lumber, automobiles and scrap metal and fertilizer, explosives and people—a vast jumble of everything, and always room for one more, Virginia.

The caboose slid past, the barriers rose and Virginia sat back in the seat, her eyes shining, her breathing accelerated. The train had excited her—its possibilities, its destination, its very movement. Impulsively, she raised her hand and waved at the caboose as it disappeared down the track.

EIGHT

Meecham stopped the car in the driveway and got out. Pulling his overcoat collar up around his neck, he went around the back of the car and opened the door for Virginia. "Here you are. And good luck."

She glanced up at him in surprise. "Aren't you coming in?"

"No."

"But my mother will want to see you, to thank you."

"She hasn't anything to thank me for. The whole thing has been a pleasure."

"You're sore, aren't you? Just because I suggested that about the bill."

"I'm not sore," Meecham said. "I have to go back to the jail to see Loftus."

"Why?"

"Because he asked me to."

"But why should he...?"

"I don't know, and I probably wouldn't tell you anyway."

"Well, thanks for the ride." She got out of the car and went toward the front door of the house. Before she was halfway there the door opened and Mrs. Hamilton came out.

Virginia ran into her mother's arms and her mother held her there, rocking back and forth. It was almost an exact repetition of the scene the previous morning in Cordwink's office.

"Momma!"

"Ginny darling. Darling girl."

"Oh, *momma!*"

Meecham watched them, but this time he felt quite detached, unmoved. He wondered what Mrs. Hamilton would do if she found out how and why Virginia had tried to raise money.

As unobtrusively as possible he slid in behind the wheel of his car and pressed the starter button. Mrs. Hamilton's reaction to the sound was immediate and exaggerated, like an amateur actress's response to a cue that was late in coming.

"Mr. Meecham! Oh, Mr. Meecham, wait a minute."

With an air of resignation Meecham switched off the ignition, set the emergency brake and got out of the car for the second time.

Mrs. Hamilton approached him, her right hand stretched out in greeting. "You weren't leaving?"

"I was. I have some bus—"

"Please come in and have a cup of coffee. Or a drink. Business can wait. This is such a happy occasion for me. I have my girl back safe and sound."

Safe and sound. Meecham almost winced at the phrase, it seemed so incongruous. Her girl would probably never be either safe or sound. He had a suspicion that Mrs. Hamilton knew this and that the phrase had slipped out, in unconscious irony.

"I'd like some coffee," Meecham said. "Nice of you to invite me."

Virginia had gone ahead into the house. Her coat had fallen off one shoulder and the hem dragged in the dirty snow.

"She looks terrible," Mrs. Hamilton said, in a changed voice. "As if she hasn't eaten, hasn't slept."

"Have you?"

"Some. Thank God it's all over now, anyway. It is over. Isn't it?"

"Yes."

"The man is guilty, he's proved it?"

"As far as I know, yes. I'm not the Sheriff's confidant."

The answer seemed to satisfy her. "I think you've brought us luck, Mr. Meecham."

The inside of the house was moist and fragrant, like a florist's shop. Meecham saw that, in anticipation of Virginia's arrival, someone had watered all the plants, watered them too liberally as if to make up for past neglect. The saucers under the flowerpots were brimming and one of the ivy-planted wall brackets dripped with sharp little *pings* onto the waxed concrete floor.

Mrs. Hamilton didn't notice the dripping. She had taken Virginia's coat and was hanging it in the closet. She handled the coat with a kind of nervous tenderness as if it was of great value and she wasn't sure how to treat it. For the first time Meecham took a close look at the coat. Its bold black and white design dazzled the eye, but the material was cheap.

Neither of the women made any move to take Meecham's hat or coat, so he laid them across a chair. He was a little irritated because he was sure that the omission on their part was more than a lapse in manners; it was an unconscious expression of their real feeling toward him. He wondered again why Mrs. Hamilton had invited him in for coffee, and why he had accepted against his will.

"We should do something to celebrate," Mrs. Hamilton said. "Perhaps a little dinner party tonight. Would you like that, Ginny?"

Virginia ignored, or didn't hear, the question. She was gazing at Meecham thoughtfully, part of her lower lip caught between her teeth. "Meecham, I've got an idea."

"Mr. Meecham, dear," Mrs. Hamilton corrected. "Mr. It sounds coarse to…"

"Momma, *please*. I'm talking."

"Then talk properly."

"Oh, for heaven's sake, Momma, this is important!" She turned back to Meecham. "I think I'll sue them for false arrest. I suffered grievous humiliation, didn't I, my reputation was damaged, I underwent great privations, et cetera. How about that, Meecham?"

"It's not such a good idea," Meecham said.

"It is, it's a wonderful idea. Why, I could get a fortune if I won."

"You couldn't win because you haven't a case. There was no malicious persecution, and the Sheriff had enough grounds to arr—"

"Stop." Mrs. Hamilton spoke quietly but with such force, such cold anger, that Meecham stopped in the middle of a word, and Virginia turned to look at her mother with an air of surprise. "I'm ashamed of you, Virginia. Ashamed."

"For heaven's sake, Momma, I've got my rights and…"

"There'll be no further discussion of this, ever." Mrs. Hamilton's face had changed from white to pink, and now back to white again, as if there was something the matter with her circulatory system and it responded too quickly and too violently to changes in her emotions. "The subject will never be brought up again. Is that clear to you, Virginia? And you, Mr. Meecham?"

"The whole thing was a pipedream anyway," Meecham said.

"Of course. Of course it was." She was regaining her composure. "You hear that, Virginia?"

"I heard."

"Now go and say hello to Carney, like a good girl. She can't leave the office."

Virginia turned obediently and walked away, but not before giving Meecham an obvious we'll-talk-about-it-later glance. Mrs. Hamilton must have seen the glance and interpreted it, but she said nothing about it until she and Meecham were settled in front of the fireplace.

Between them, so close to Meecham that he could scarcely move his legs, there was an immense three-tiered glass table that looked as though it weighed a ton. The chair that Meecham occupied was deep and low and soft, one of those chairs it was difficult to get out of even without a table blocking the way.

Meecham felt suddenly and inexplicably afraid. The fear passed over him like a wave, accelerating his heartbeat, and left behind beads of moisture on his forehead and a damp cold sensation across the small of his back. He had to control an impulse to kick away the huge table, spilling the coffee from its silver urn, shattering the china cups and the glass tiers. Violence is the instinctive response to fear. But because the fear was nameless and unimmediate, the violence was vague and unreasoning. He dropped an ash tray. Dropped it, quite unintentionally, and when he saw it break he had no conscious feeling of satisfaction, but he stopped sweating and his heartbeat was normal again.

Mrs. Hamilton dismissed his apologies with a gesture. She looked annoyed, not at the loss of the ash tray, but at the interruption of her thoughts.

She said quietly and firmly, "You understand, don't you, that Virginia gets wild ideas sometimes. You mustn't take them seriously."

"I don't."

"This false arrest business would never do, you understand that."

"Quite." He didn't remind her that he'd said the same thing himself, at least twice.

"Virginia can be very persuasive. I—I *beg* of you not to pay any attention to her. She doesn't realize the consequences of such a thing—more publicity and investigations, policemen prying into things."

"What things?"

"Everything," she said, spreading her small plump hands.

"Paul has suffered enough. Crank phone calls and letters, and reporters stopping him on the street."

"It will all blow over."

"Not if Virginia does anything further. Like this suit she wants to start."

"No lawyer would touch it."

It was his third or fourth reassurance. "That's a relief," she said, and Meecham thought the subject was closed until she added, "Why does Virginia want money so badly?"

"You'd better ask her."

"She'd lie."

"Maybe."

"Not that she's a liar, a real liar, but she's secretive sometimes because she doesn't understand how completely sympathetic I am to her." She repeated the word *completely* with emphasis, as if denying an unspoken accusation of lack of sympathy. "I understand her, she's my girl. We've always been very close."

"I see that."

"Tell me frankly, Mr. Meecham. Did you examine any of the reports about Virginia?"

"What reports?"

"While she was in—while she was there, they must have asked her questions, given her tests, things like that. They usually do, don't they?"

"Yes."

"You don't know how they—turned out?"

"No."

"I thought since you were... Well, it doesn't really matter. Virginia's normal, of course. A little spoiled, but completely normal."

"I agree," Meecham said. It was futile to say anything else.

Mrs. Hamilton looked at him gratefully. She had received the answer she wanted and now it was time to change the subject before Meecham could reverse or modify his answer. She said, "It's been a sordid business. I'm glad it's over, and I suppose you are too."

"In a way."

"Send me your bill as soon as possible. I don't know how long I'll be staying here. Or I can pay you right now, if you like, in cash."

"That won't be necessary."

Somewhere in the house a telephone rang, twice.

"You'll come to our little celebration dinner tonight, Mr. Meecham?"

"Thanks, but I'm afraid I won't be able to make it." He never wanted to set foot in that house again, to be subtly imprisoned by a soft chair and a glass table and a quiet frantic woman. "I have some business to attend to."

"Of course. You must have other clients, hundreds."

"A few, anyway."

"This man, Loftus. He'll undoubtedly get a good lawyer?"

"Money or no money, he'll get a lawyer of some kind."

"Why do you say, money or no money?"

"If he can't afford to pay, the court will appoint two lawyers for the defense. There's no Public Defender here as there is in Los Angeles."

"I didn't realize we had such a thing. I've never had occasion to be interested in—matters like that."

Quick light footsteps sounded in the hall, and a moment later Alice appeared in the doorway. She looked as if she had been working. Her hair was drawn back tightly behind her ears and tied with a blue ribbon, and she wore an apron that reached almost to her ankles. Her face was warm and flushed and pretty.

Mrs. Hamilton frowned, faintly but pointedly, in Alice's direction, like a mother silencing a little girl, warning her not to interrupt while the grownups were talking. Or, if she had to interrupt, at least to remove her apron first.

"My dear Alice," she said, "what have you been doing?"

"Cleaning."

"You know perfectly well you're not expected to do any of the household work."

"I don't mind. And it needed doing."

Mrs. Hamilton turned to Meecham with a smile that seemed forced. "Now what would you do with a girl like that?"

"I don't know," Meecham said. He felt, quite irrationally, that Alice's appearance had changed something in the room, broken a tension, snapped an invisible wire. He got up from the chair, pushing the glass table away until its bamboo legs shrieked in protest. The table was lighter than he thought.

Alice was watching him gravely from the doorway. "Your office called, Mr. Meecham. You're to drop in there after you talk to Mr. Loftus."

"Thank you."

In the silence that followed Meecham could hear the ivy-planted wall bracket still dripping, very slowly and softly, like the final blood from a death wound.

Mrs. Hamilton had risen too, to face Meecham. "I think you might be quite a clever and devious creature, Mr. Meecham."

"So is a weasel, so I won't bother thanking you for that, Mrs. Hamilton."

"You've been stringing me along," she said in a cold flat voice. "*You're* going to be Loftus' lawyer, aren't you?"

"No."

"You can lie about it. Go on. Everybody else lies."

"I'm not lying."

"How can I believe you? How can I believe anybody?" She crossed the room, moving with agonizing slowness like a deep-sea diver forcing his leaden feet across the ocean floor, fighting a pressure he can't see or understand. "I... Alice, I think I'll go up to my room and rest awhile. Please see that Mr. Meecham is—looked after."

Meecham watched her until she disappeared around a corner of the hall. Then he turned his head and looked at Alice, and in that moment he had two wishes, diverging in means, but with a common purpose: to get Alice away from that house. His first wish was that he had a mother or a father or a family of some kind so that he could invite Alice to stay with them. Since he had no family at all, he wished that Mrs. Hamilton would take Alice and board the earliest plane for home. Some day, some remote day when he had surplus time and money, he might go to see her. She might be married, by that time, married and with a couple of children; a placid contented matron, shopping, going to movies, lying in the sun. This projection into the future was so vivid, his sense of loss so acute, that he felt a tide of rage rise in him, rise and ebb, leaving a taste of salt.

He said, abruptly, "When are you leaving for home?"

"You mean L.A.?"

"Yes."

"I don't know. Mrs. Hamilton hasn't told me."

"You could tell her. Tell her you want to leave."

"But I don't want to," she protested.

"Have you seen Virginia?"

"Yes, a few minutes ago, with Carney."

"Suppose I told you I think Virginia is dangerous?"

"Are you trying to scare me? I don't understand. Everything is all right now, isn't it? Everything's been settled?" She took a step back, away from him. "Or has it? Why are you going to see Loftus if you're not his lawyer?"

"Because he asked me to."

"As an old pal?"

"More or less."

"You never saw him before last night, does that make you an old pal?"

"He thought I had an honest face," Meecham said, "so I became his old pal right away. It happens, now and then, especially to a lonely guy in trouble. I'm a lonely guy myself and I've been in trouble, so I know a little about these things." He put on his coat. "Nobody seems to like the idea of me talking to Loftus. I wonder why."

"I don't care, one way or the other. I was just puzzled." She thrust her hands deep into the pockets of the oversize apron. "I guess I'm getting suspicious of everybody. I don't know why."

"That's the trouble with suspicion, it infects even the nicest people. Goodbye, Alice."

"Goodbye."

He bent down and kissed her lightly on the forehead. She didn't react in any way. She just stood there, looking surprised and a little forlorn.

He was halfway to the center of town before he realized that he hadn't had any coffee after all. He wanted, then, to turn around and go back, not for the coffee he had missed, but because the solution of the problem had suddenly struck him. It was quite simple: the house should be abandoned like a ship about to sink under the weight of excess cargo. Alice and Mrs. Hamilton should go home, Carney get another job, Paul rent an office somewhere downtown. And Virginia—there was only one thing to do about Virginia: give her the money to run away, far away where the climate was good.

He thought of the expression on her face as she had watched the train go past and waved at the red caboose. Motion, change, speed, they were essential to Virginia. She should always be on a passing train, one that went round and round the world and never stopped.

NINE

Meecham didn't go directly to the jail. The place he wanted to see first was on his way. He found it finally, after driving past twice—a small store with a single window, wedged inconspicuously between a bowling alley and a cigar shop.

A sign above the door was lettered in green and white: Doug Devine, Prop. There was no other identification, and none was needed. The window was piled to the ceiling with the scraps and leavings, the hopes and futilities, the desires and fears and evils, of human beings. Wedding rings and automatics, rosaries and hunting knives, worn shoes and violins; and, at the back of the window, the bland, ageless face of a grandfather clock. The clock was running, and on time: 10:35.

Inside the store a middle-aged man was sitting on a wicker bench examining a shotgun. The gun was old and grimy. About four or five inches of the barrel had been sawed off, and the rest of it was mended with black friction tape. It was a desperate weapon, as likely to explode when the trigger was pulled as to discharge its shot. Meecham wondered what desperate man had bought and sold it, and what desperate man would buy it and add another chapter to its dark allusive history.

Devine looked up from his task. He was a black Irishman with coarse curly hair and eyes bright as beetles. "It works," he said briefly. "I tried it."

"Oh?"

"Sure. But you never know what you're going to hit. Aim it at your wife and you end up shooting the neighbor's pet goldfish."

"That could be good."

"Oh, sure. No argument about that. No law against shooting up goldfish." He got up and put the shotgun carefully on the wicker bench. "Anything I can do for you?"

"Maybe."

"Buying or selling?"

"Buying."

"I figure you for an insurance investigator," Devine said. "Right or wrong?"

"Wrong."

"I bet I was close."

"Pretty close."

"I'm always close. Practically the only thing I know in this whole cockeyed world is people and I can't make a nickel out of it. Give me an idea what you're interested in. You want to start music lessons, we got a nice clarinet."

"No, thanks. What I..."

"Fellow that sold it to me said it once belonged to Benny Goodman. Funny thing, how a lot of people dream up the same old stuff and think it's new. There's not a clarinet in any pawnshop east of Frisco that ain't been played by Goodman or Artie Shaw. We got some nice bargains in jewelry."

"I was thinking of a picture frame."

"Just the frame?"

"Yes."

"We got some first-class framed oil paintings, some genuine Manderheims."

"I never heard of Manderheim."

"I never did either, but you'd be surprised how many I've sold." He pointed to a picture of a vase of roses and ivy that was propped against the legs of an up-ended chair. "See that, over there. If I told my customers that somebody's Aunt Agnes painted it on her kitchen table, I couldn't give it away. But Manderheim—well, he's different, he's strictly class. Romantic, even. You want to know why he doesn't sign his pictures? Well, he's run away with another man's wife, see, and he doesn't want to be recognized because the husband is out gunning for him. Yes, sir, people will believe anything if it's preposterous enough." He added, with a touch of gloom, "Funny thing is, I damn near believe in Manderheim myself."

So did Meecham. "Maybe some other time I'll take a Manderheim," he said. "Right now all I want is a frame. My girl-friend had her picture taken last week. By a curious coincidence her name's Manderheim too."

Devine didn't smile. "You want a *silver* frame?"

"Yes."

"About eight by ten?"

"About that."

Devine was silent a moment, rubbing the side of his chin with his hand. His skin was like sandpaper. "I'm in a peculiar business, mister, and I get peculiar people in here asking for peculiar things. Now there's nothing special about a silver picture frame by itself. I buy one occasionally, sell one occasionally. What's peculiar is that this morning, inside of one little hour, I get three calls for a silver frame. You're the third. The second was a cop, and the first was a lady."

"Who was she?"

"State your business, mister."

Meecham took one of his professional cards from his wallet.

Devine accepted the card, read it with a grunt and dropped it on the floor. "I told the cop, and I'm telling you. I didn't know her from Adam."

"You said people are your specialty. You must have noticed her."

"Sure, sure. I figured her for a nurse, or maybe a schoolteacher. She was ordinary, not bad-looking not good-looking, not well-dressed, not poorly dressed. Forty, or thereabouts, thin, had a sharp nose. Looked like she'd been crying or had a bad cold. She was standing outside when I opened up the store at nine. She said she wanted a few odds and ends for her house, and would I mind if she looked around. She went through the whole place very methodically, like someone who's used to looking for things. It took her about twenty minutes to find what she wanted: the silver frame, a table radio, and an onyx pen and pencil set. $48.50 for the works. A steal."

"Have you seen the papers this morning?"

"I've got four kids," Devine said. "When you got four kids you don't read the paper until night when they're all in bed. Why?"

Meecham ignored the question. "I suppose you remember who sold you the articles that this woman bought."

"Certainly. I both remember and I got it written down on my books. He's a young man I've done business with before. Sometimes he pawns a couple things, sometimes sells them outright like yesterday. His name's Desmond. Duane Desmond." He studied Meecham's face for a moment. "That's a phony, eh? I kind of thought it might be. What's his real tag?"

"Earl Loftus."

"Why all the sudden interest in him? He dead or something?"

"He's in jail."

"Is that a fact?" Devine showed no surprise. "Well, like they say, it couldn't happen to a nicer guy. Who was the lady who bought the stuff he sold me?"

"I thought you might have recognized her," Meecham said with a wry little smile. "It was Manderheim's mistress."

Devine blushed like a girl. "Oh, can it now. What the hell." He followed Meecham to the door. "The stuff I got from Desmond—Loftus, I mean—it wasn't hot?"

"No."

"That's a relief. I wonder why the woman bought it all back again?"

"Maybe to return it to him." Maybe to remember him by, he added silently. He thought of the way she had sat in Loftus' room, her head buried in her hands, in silent grief. He said, "There was no picture in the frame?"

"Sure there was. A nice-looking woman, sixty or thereabouts, white hair. I figured at first it must be Loftus' mother. I asked him didn't he want to take the picture out and keep it, and he said no. So I guess it wasn't his mother."

"I think it was."

"Well, now that's strange, eh? You'd think a guy would keep a picture of his own mother."

It was strange. Particularly strange in the case of Loftus, the devoted son. "What did you do with it?"

"Threw it away. It was no pin-up, what else would I do?"

"Maybe you could remember where you threw it."

"Sure I could remember, for all the good it will do. I put it in the furnace and burned it along with the other rubbish. It was just an ordinary picture, ordinary woman. How was I to know anybody'd want it? What do you want it for, anyway?"

"I don't. I'm just curious. I'd like to know why Loftus didn't keep it."

"Maybe he was sore at her. I get sore at my old lady."

"You may be right." Meecham opened the door. After the mustiness of the shop the winter wind felt fresh and clean. "Thanks for the information."

"Welcome. Come in again."

"I will." Meecham stepped out into the street and stood for a moment in front of the cluttered window, buttoning his topcoat. When he looked back into the store, he saw that Devine had returned to the wicker bench and was sitting with the ancient shotgun across his knees.

TEN

He found Loftus in a small room across the hall from the Sheriff's office. Loftus was alone, and not under restraint of any kind, though there was a policeman outside in the corridor.

Meecham knew the policeman. His name was Samuels; he was nearing retirement age, his legs and feet bothered him, and he suffered from attacks of hiccups that sometimes lasted for hours. Whenever Samuels got the hiccups his colleagues planned intricate, and occasionally hilarious, ways of scaring them away. None of them worked.

"Hello, Samuels," Meecham said. "How are things?"

"Bad. You got here just in time. They're taking your boy in there away."

"Where to?"

"The doc says he should be in a hospital. So as soon as I get the transfer papers, that's where I'm taking him, out to County."

"I'll talk to him first. Mind if I close this door?"

Samuels shrugged, a magnificently eloquent shrug which implied that as far as he was concerned every door in the place should be shut and the whole building blown up.

Meecham went inside and closed the door. The room was very small, furnished with a card table and three folding chairs, all different, a bridge lamp, a davenport with two broken springs, and a swivel chair with a cracked and worn leather seat. Everything in the room seemed to be discards from other rooms and offices, including the pictures that lined the windowless walls: photographs of the Detroit Red Wings, Abraham Lincoln, a sailboat,

Dizzy Dean, and a score of unnamed and unremembered magistrates and judges and policemen.

Loftus was sitting in one of the folding chairs, staring up at the ceiling ventilator, his eyes strained and supplicating, as if they saw, beyond the ventilator, the sky; and beyond the sky the great hole of eternity already open for him.

Meecham said, "Loftus?"

Loftus moaned, faintly, the protesting sound of a man returning from a dream.

"Sorry I'm late, Loftus. Are you feeling all right?"

"I've been trying to pray. My mind won't let me, it keeps flying, flying through space." He lowered his head, and his eyes met Meecham's. "They're taking me away. I think I'm dying."

The ventilator whirred like wings.

"No. No, you're not, Loftus. Cordwink thinks you'll be more comfortable in the hospital, have more care, better food." He spoke too heartily, in an attempt to cover his conviction that the care and comfort were too late, the food useless to a man who couldn't eat.

"I don't want to go to the hospital. Please. I don't want to go, Mr. Meecham."

"I can't prevent them doing what's best for you."

"It's not best. I hate that air, smelling of sickness. I—well, I'll go, of course. I'll go. There's no choice." He glanced down at the suitcase beside his feet. It was the first time Meecham noticed it. "Emmy came to see me this morning."

"Mrs. Hearst?"

"Yes. They wouldn't let her in, but they let me have the stuff she brought me, some of my clothes and my radio. I don't know how she got the radio. I sold it yesterday."

"She bought it back from Devine this morning."

"She? God! She must have found out about the name I—I used."

"Maybe not," Meecham said. "I did, though."

"Duane Desmond. How do you like that for a grown man, eh? Funny, isn't it? I don't know what got into me. Duane Desmond. God!" He pounded the flimsy card table with his fist. One of the hinged legs collapsed and the table sagged but didn't fall. Loftus bent down and straightened the hinge, looking a little ashamed of himself. "You won't tell Emmy."

"Why should I?"

"She mustn't find out. She doesn't know I'm a fool." He rested his head on his hands. Meecham saw then the toothmarks on the knuckles of both of Loftus' hands. Even in the dim yellow light of the old bridge lamp they were plainly the marks of teeth, and one of them was bleeding. The blood looked like any other blood to Meecham. But he knew that this blood was venom, and that the long night—when Loftus had sat in silent frenzy biting his knuckles—was only the beginning of a longer night.

Meecham was seized by a sensation of incredible helplessness. He wanted to communicate with Loftus, to express sympathy and friendship, but the words he knew were inadequate as all words are inadequate in the imminence of death. For the first time in his life Meecham experienced a sense of religion, a feeling that the only way he and Loftus could communicate with each other was through a third being, a translator of the spirit.

Loftus turned his head suddenly. "You went to Devine's to check up on me, Mr. Meecham?"

"I had to find out what happened to the articles that were missing from your room, whether you'd given them away, pawned them, sold them."

"Is that so important?"

104

"It's important because Cordwink has—or had—an idea that someone paid you to kill Margolis."

"Is that your idea too?"

"No. I think you sold the stuff to Devine because you were broke. If you were broke, obviously you weren't paid."

"I could have told you that."

"Certainly. You could tell me anything you like but it wouldn't necessarily be the truth."

"You think I'm a liar, Mr. Meecham?" he said, anxiously.

"You're human."

"All this checking up on me, it's not necessary. I ask no favors. I'm a guilty man and I'm willing to take my punishment. But this prying—this unnecessary..."

"What you say isn't evidence unless it's backed by what you've done."

"I guess you're right. But whatever you find out, don't tell Emmy."

"What is there to find out?"

Loftus didn't answer. He was gnawing on his bleeding knuckles again.

"She's very fond of you, Loftus."

"She is, yes, I'm sure she is. I... What did...? You were talking to her last night, what did she say about me?"

"She was full of praise, of course; how kind and thoughtful you were, and a little bit about your history."

Footsteps passed in the corridor beyond the door. They sounded faint and far away.

"It's hard to admit you're nothing," Loftus said. "I'm admitting it now. My life has been without meaning or purpose or satisfaction. I should never have been born; my father didn't want children and my mother felt trapped by the responsibility. The whole thing has been a mistake from beginning to end. I am afraid of my moment of dying, terribly afraid. But I will be glad to be gone. You don't read poetry, Mr. Meecham?"

"No."

"There's a phrase that Yeats used. I have it written down in my book." He took a little black notebook from his shirt pocket and leafed through it. Each page that Meecham could see was crammed from top to bottom with writing, writing so small that it seemed impossible to read with the naked eye. He wondered whether this was Loftus' natural handwriting, or whether he wrote that way deliberately to save space in the little book.

"Here it is," Loftus said. "I'm not sure exactly what it means, it's out of context. But this one phrase keeps cropping up in my head lately: 'That this pragmatical preposterous pig of a world, its farrow that so solid seem, Must vanish on the instant if the mind but change its theme.'

"'Pragmatical preposterous pig of a world,'" he said, spitting out the words like pits that he'd been chewing too long. "That describes it. I will be glad to leave."

He lapsed into silence again. The only sound in the room was the whirring of the ventilator, though there was a sensation of sound and movement, as if beyond the closed door many things were happening, preposterous things.

Meecham said, "Why did you ask me to come here?"

"I want to hire you. Oh, not to defend me, that won't be necessary. But there are one or two little things that I won't be able to take care of. I'd like you to do them for me."

"What are they?"

"I have some money. I sold my car and a few little articles. It amounted to $716.00 I want my mother to have it."

"Where is it?"

"Emmy will give it to you. It's in an envelope in the middle of a package of letters. Deduct your fee, whatever it is, and give the rest of the money and all the letters to my mother. They're her letters. She wrote them to me when I came here. Tell her..." He hesitated, clenching and unclenching his hands. "Tell her to reread them, every one of them, to see... No. No, don't tell her that. Let her do what she likes with them. It's too late anyway. Just give her the money and tell her to go away somewhere for a while."

"Why?"

"She can't—can't face things very well. It's better if she goes away. Her address was in one of the morning papers. That's bad. She may be hounded by reporters or—well, Kincaid is a small cruel town."

"I'll deliver your message. I don't guarantee that I can persuade her to leave."

"You can try. Here, I'll write the address down for you."

"Don't bother, I saw the papers," Meecham said. He remembered the address, not from any newspaper, but from the Railway Express consignment slip that had been pasted across Loftus' suitcase: FROM MRS. CHARLES E. LOFTUS, 231 OAK STREET, KINCAID, MICHIGAN, TO MR. EARL DUANE LOFTUS, 611 DIVISION STREET, ARBANA, MICHIGAN. CONTENTS VALUED AT $50.00.

"I know it's asking a lot, Mr. Meecham. But if you could go sometime today, get to her first—it's only a hundred miles..."

"I'll go today."

"Thank you." Loftus rose, clumsily, supporting himself by leaning one hand on the card table and the other on the back of the chair. "Thank you very much."

"Why didn't you keep her picture, Loftus?"

"I wanted to be alone. Entirely alone, without even a picture. Can you understand that?"

"It isn't a good thing to be alone. Relatives have a way of standing by in emergencies. Haven't you got any, except your mother?"

"I had a wife once. She left me, got a divorce. I can't blame her. She was a big, strong, healthy woman. At least she was then, I haven't seen her for a long time."

"Has it occurred to you that your mother might want to come here to see you?"

Loftus shrugged, wearily. "She won't come. Oh, she'll want to come, she may even plan to come, have everything arranged, suitcase neatly packed, everything. She may even get as far as the bus depot. Then she'll take a little drink to calm her nerves. You can guess the rest."

"Yes." He recalled the number of books about alcoholism that Loftus kept in his room.

"She was always death against liquor. She never had a drink until she was nearly fifty. My father had run out on her by that time, and one day she went out and bought a bottle of wine to calm her nerves. It happened right away. One drink, and she was a drunk. She'd been a drunk for maybe thirty years and didn't find it out until then. For her the world vanished in that instant. She has never seen it since. She never will again."

"Perhaps. There are cures."

Loftus only shook his head.

"I'll see to it personally that she comes to visit you, if you want her to."

"No, thank you," Loftus said politely. "I don't want to see anyone."

The door from the corridor opened and the policeman, Samuels, came in. He had taken his handcuffs from the leather case fastened to his belt and he was playing with them, clicking them from wide to narrow and back again, the way Miss Jennings played with her ring of keys and for the same reason, because he was bored and a little embarrassed.

"All through, Mr. Meecham? We got orders to be on the move."

Meecham turned to Loftus. "Are we all through?"

"I think so," Loftus said.

"If something else comes up, let me know. In any case, I'll be around to see you when I've transacted the business we discussed. Perhaps early in the morning."

"Thank you."

"I'll see Emmy right away."

"Tell her not to worry. Everything's going to be fine."

"I will. Good luck."

Meecham stood in the doorway of the small windowless room and watched the two men go down the corridor, handcuffed together, walking slowly and in step. Then he turned, abruptly, and walked as fast as he could in the other direction and out the rear entrance.

It was noon, but there was no sun. The sky hung close over the smoky city like a sagging tent top that would some day blow away, exposing the vast blackness of space.

Meecham waited for the traffic signal to change. A car went through the yellow light and almost sideswiped another car. Both drivers began to curse, ineffectually through closed windows, like little boys hurling threats from the safety of their own doorsteps. A woman came out of the supermarket across the street, jerking the arm of the crying child staggering along behind her. An old man on crutches inched his way across the icy sidewalk to the curb and stood eyeing the speeding cars with hate and fear.

A column of bitterness rose like mercury in Meecham's throat. *Pig of a world*, he thought. *Preposterous pig of a world.*

ELEVEN

When he rang the doorbell Emmy Hearst answered it herself, immediately, as if she'd been there at the door watching from behind the lace curtains of the little window for someone who would never come. Her eyes were so swollen that they didn't look like human eyes at all, but like twin blisters raised by fire. When she spoke she held one hand against her throat as if to ease its aching:

"You saw him?"

Meecham nodded. "Yes."

"I tried to. They wouldn't let me. They said I had no right, no right." She clung to the door for support, a tall strong woman who had come abruptly, in a single day, to the end of her strength.

"They've transferred him to the hospital," Meecham said.

"He'll get good care there. Won't he?"

"Of course."

There was a burst of masculine laughter from one of the rooms on the second floor.

Mrs. Hearst glanced nervously at the staircase. "I can't ask you to come in, I—I'm busy. I have business to attend to."

Meecham said, "I can't stay anyway. Loftus asked me to pick up a package of letters that he wants me to take to his mother."

"His mother," she said quietly. "Always his mother. She's a stone around his neck, drowning him, she's like a… Yes, I have the letters. They're in the kitchen. I'll get them for you."

She went down the hall and through the swinging door into the kitchen. Meecham heard her give a little cry of surprise: "Why—why, I thought you were upstairs."

"Well, I'm not upstairs. How do you like that, eh?"

The door stopped swinging and settled into place, entombing the sound waves in its heavy oak. But the woman's little cry of surprise hung in the air for a moment like a question mark of smoke and then disintegrated.

Meecham waited, uneasy and depressed. The front door was still open and he didn't close it; he felt that she had left it open deliberately. The wind blew down the hall and up the stairs, agitating the lace curtains and the coats and sweaters hanging on the old-fashioned hall rack. On the floor beside the rack there was a pile of rubbers and galoshes and a pair of battered tube skates and one gym shoe with the name Kryboski inked on each side.

Meecham looked at his watch and then coughed, a long purposeful cough. A minute later the swinging door opened again and Mrs. Hearst came toward him with a brown package under her arm. She was lurching slightly, as if she was carrying either inside the package or inside herself something heavy that threw her off balance.

She thrust the package at him. It was very light. "Here. Please go. *Please.*"

"Certainly," Meecham said. But he was a little too late. A man had come out of the kitchen, a big ruddy-faced man with fair hair. A hall-length away he looked quite distinguished and physically powerful. But as he came nearer, the shaft of light from the open door exposed the fraud like an efficient camera. His body was running to fat, and his face was disfigured by lines of indecision and self-doubt, ambition gone sour and life gone sour. His pale eyes moved constantly, back and forth, like birds at sea looking for a piece of kelp to rest on. He was one of those men Meecham recognized as a common type; the big boy whose mind and emotions had never been able to keep up with his maturing body.

With the years the gap widened and the personality narrowed. He was, perhaps, forty-five.

Mrs. Hearst deliberately turned her head away as he approached. When she spoke she didn't look at either of the men, she seemed to be addressing the grease-darkened lilies that climbed the wall: "This is my husband, Jim."

"Say, what is all this anyhow?" Hearst said. "Just what is it? Mysterious packages, cops in the house, Emmy bawling all over the joint. A guy has a right to know, don't he?"

He tugged, self-consciously, at his tie. The checked suit he wore was a little too tight around the hips, and the sleeves were too short, so that his wrists stuck out, not the vulnerable pipe-stem wrists of a growing boy, but thick wrists covered with coarse gold hairs. His manner, his clothes, his expression, they all added to his air of chronic failure... the air of a man who has tried and quit a hundred jobs in a hundred places, always out of step and off-beat.

"Well? Ain't anybody going to say anything but me? Not that I can't do the talking. I've got plenty to say and plenty to ask too."

"Shut up, Jim," Mrs. Heart said, without turning.

"Now she tells me, shut up. Mind my own business, she says. Maybe that's my trouble, I have minded my own business. I've winked an eye at things." He looked at his wife. "Some pretty funny things, eh, Emmy?"

"Shut up," she repeated listlessly. "He's not a cop, he's a lawyer. And the package... Oh, you tell him, Mr. Meecham. Tell him what's in the package since he won't believe me."

"They're letters," Meecham said. "Written to Loftus by his mother. I'm returning them to her at his request."

Hearst looked disappointed. "Just a bunch of old letters, eh?"

"That's right."

"You mean all the value they've got is just sentimental?"

"Yes." Meecham didn't mention the money in one of the envelopes. He had the notion that if Hearst knew there was money involved he would put up a fight to keep it; a not unreasonable fight, since the package had been left in his own kitchen, and he, Meecham, had no power of attorney for Loftus, and, in fact, no proof that the package even belonged to Loftus.

But Hearst had already lost interest in the package. He was watching his wife, his eyes moving constantly in their sockets but keeping her within range. "He's quite a sentimental guy, Loftus is. Too bad I don't have that sentimental stuff, the ladies are crazy for it. And manners he's got too, real fancy manners that makes an ordinary guy feel like a bum. I'm not a bum. I'm a rough diamond, sure, but I don't go around carving people up either. Eh, Emmy?"

"I don't know what you do when you're out of town," she said distinctly. "And I don't care."

"I work. That's what I do. I *work*." The word seemed to stimulate him. He turned to Meecham, suddenly animated: "Right now I'm pushing a new product we got out, a soapless suds. Best thing on the market, Noscrub it's called. I'm in charge of out-of-town advertising."

"You distribute free samples from door to door," his wife said, still speaking in the same clear and distinct way, like a teacher correcting the repeated lies of a small boy.

"That's right, build me up. That's great. Funny how you could get so mealy-mouthed over Loftus because he read books instead of doing a man's work. Books and soft talk…"

"A man's work. A two-year-old could be taught to deliver samples from door to door."

His face purpled and he seemed ready to strike her. He looked, for the first time, decisive, sure of his ground and his rights. But the moment passed. His anger, like his other emotions, was not quite fully developed; it turned against himself so that he was his own victim.

"Wait till the product catches on," he said. "Just wait."

"Yes, Jim."

"I'll be advertising manager, I've got Weber's word for it."

"Yes, Jim."

"Yes Jim, yes Jim, yes Jim." He shook his head, in a new anger and an old despair. "Goddam it, build me up, Emmy. Like a real wife, build me up."

"The higher you're built the sooner you'll fall."

"You built *him* up. Earl this, Earl that, Earl you're wonderful."

"I never said he was wonderful."

"You did. I heard you."

"People who spy at doors will hear anything, and what they don't hear they'll make up."

"I didn't have to spy at doors. It was here, all over the place, right under my nose." His eyes shifted to Meecham. "How about that, eh? You take a guy into your home, you treat him right, treat him like your own…"

"You never said a civil word to him in your life." She was examining the wallpaper again. "Not a civil word."

"You said enough for both of us, didn't you? What do you think, I should of shook his hand for making me feel like an old bum?"

"I haven't had a friend since I left school, man or woman, not a friend. That's what Earl is to me, a friend."

"I've kicked around in my life, and one thing I know, there's no such thing as a man and woman being friends. It's not in the books. It's against nature."

"Your nature, maybe. Not…"

"Anybody's nature!"

"Keep your voice down. The boys might hear you."

"Let them. Maybe they'll learn a thing or two."

"If you don't mind," Meecham said, "I'd better be going."

Neither of them paid the slightest attention. They were absorbed in each other, like boxers in a ring, each of them intent only on the other's weak spots and unguarded moments.

She had crossed her arms on her chest, as if protecting a vulnerable place. "What are you accusing me of? Say it."

"I will."

"Well, go on. Say it in front of Mr. Meecham here. He's a lawyer."

"Sure, I'll say it. I don't care if he's President Truman."

"Well, what's stopping you? Go on, go on."

"He was your lover," Hearst said. "That piddling little shrimp was your lover."

"You fool," she whispered. "You *terrible* fool." She began to cry, very quietly, her forehead pressing against the wall. Tears fell from her swollen eyes and splattered the greasy lilies of the wallpaper. Her head moved, from one side to another, in misery and denial.

"Emmy?"

"Go away."

"It's not true then, eh, Emmy?"

"What do you think? A sick man—a dying man—what—do—you—think?"

"I—well…"

He looked with pathetic uncertainty at Meecham, like a small boy who had made his mother cry and sought reassurance that eventually she would stop and everything would be all right again.

"Emmy?" He touched her shoulder tentatively. "I didn't mean nothing, Emmy. You know me, I shoot off at the mouth, sure, but I wouldn't hurt a hair of your head. If you was only honest with me, Emmy. If you was only honest."

Meecham went out the door with the package under his arm. Neither of them noticed or cared.

Outside, the wind was fresh, but he had a sensation of suffocating heaviness in his throat and chest, as if the slices of life he had seen in the course of the morning were too sharp and fibrous to be swallowed.

TWELVE

Highway 12 ran due west from Arbana to Kincaid, just over fifty miles of straight road through flat countryside. Under better circumstances it might have been an hour drive. But heavy trucks and heavy weather had pocked and dented the road, and beyond Jackson the snow began to fall in huge wet flakes that clung to the windshield like glue. Every few minutes Meecham had to slow down to give the windshield wipers more power and speed.

When he reached Kincaid it was five, and the street lights were on. Here and there a few houses were already decorated for Christmas, with strings of colored lights along the porches, clusters of pine branches and cones attached to the doors. The shops and the streets were crowded, and the crowds looked gay as if freshened by the new snow.

He had no trouble finding Oak Street. It crossed the main highway at a traffic signal in the center of town.

Two Hundred Thirty-one was a two-story, white-brick apartment house in a neighborhood that derived its brash but decaying air from nearby slums. Meecham parked his car and crossed the street with the brown package under his arm. The building itself was well kept, and nailed to the front door there was a Christmas wreath, a red cellophane bell surrounded by artificial spruce boughs and red wax berries. The snow made the spruce and the berries look quite real.

Inside the small lobby there was a row of locked mailboxes and on the wall a black arrow pointing to the basement, and a sign, Manager's Office. The third mailbox belonged to Loftus' mother: Mrs. C. E. Loftus, Apartment Five.

Meecham walked down the hall. The carpeting was worn but clean, and the air smelled pungently of paint. Someone in the building obviously had a flair for lettering. All over the walls there were elaborately executed instructions: APARTMENTS ONE–FIVE, THIS WAY →→. NO SMOKING IN CORRIDORS. KEEP YOUR RADIO LOW AFTER ELEVEN O'CLOCK PLEASE. NO SOLICITING. PLEASE USE NIGHT BELL ONLY WHEN NECESSARY. NIGHT BELL ↓↓.

Number Five had a fire extinguisher fastened to the wall just outside the door. Meecham pressed the buzzer, waited half a minute, and pressed it again, twice. There was no response. He went back to the lobby and down the steps to the basement following the Manager's Office arrow.

A small man past middle age, in a peaked painting cap and splattered overalls, was squatting in a full knee bend outside the door, putting masking tape around the knob. He turned when he heard Meecham's footsteps, turned without rising and without losing his balance even for a moment. His back was straight as a board.

"Yes, sir?"

"Are you the manager?"

"Yes, sir, I am. Victor Garino."

"I'm looking for Mrs. Loftus. I'm Eric Meecham, a friend of Earl's, her son."

Garino's eyes behind his rimless spectacles looked misty.

"Oh, you are? Earl's a fine boy. You tried her apartment?"

"Yes."

"Well, come in, come inside." He opened the door and Meecham preceded him into a small living room. The room was so crowded with furniture and knickknacks that there was hardly any space to move. In a box beside an electric heater a litter of kittens was mewling, while the mother cat stalked around and around the box

118

with a kind of angry dignity, as if ashamed of the way her children were behaving in front of a stranger.

"You like cats, Mr. Meecham? Yes?"

"Very much." He had never particularly liked or disliked them but the sight of the tiny furry bodies stirred something inside him.

"Yes, I like all animals, but cats, ah, they're quiet and quick, and they earn their keep. We never have any complaints about rats," Garino added proudly. "Never. Sit down, will you? Then I can sit down too. Ah, that's better. You came from Earl, eh? How is he?"

"The same as usual."

"Ah, yes. Did you…? You knocked on her door very loud, did you? Sometimes she's hard of hearing. Also she's a deep sleeper."

"Also she gets loaded."

"Yes," Garino said in a melancholy voice. "She gets loaded very bad. Often's the time I let myself in her apartment with my passkey just to see she's not burning the place down or something. She's a problem. She's a nice lady but she's a problem."

"I can see that."

"How we found out, Mama and me, was by the incinerator. Rum bottles. Empty rum bottles kept coming down the chute all the time making a fine mess. Mama said it must be Mrs. Loftus. No, I said, no, how could it be, such a nice dignified lady drinking all that rum. Mama was right, though." Garino's eyes were sad as a hound's. "I went up and asked Mrs. Loftus please not to throw rum bottles down the chute. Right away she denied it, acted real shocked. Why, Victor, she said, why, Victor, you know I never touch the stuff. It must be the young couple upstairs, she said."

The mother cat had settled down beside Garino on the davenport and was purring in her sleep.

"After that," Garino said, "there were no more rum bottles in the incinerator. She took them out and threw them somewhere. I

119

often saw her go down the street with a paper bag full of bottles. It looked funny, her such a lady walking down the street to dispose of her *garbage*. Ah, we feel bad, Mama and me. The bottles didn't make such a great mess, we would have just let her keep on using the incinerator."

"Maybe you should."

"It's too late now. If I went and told her it was all right to use the incinerator she couldn't *pretend* any more, she couldn't have any pride left. That wouldn't be good. Anyway"—Garino spread his hands—"she's not such a terrible bother. Her rent is always paid, Earl sends it to me. And she is quiet. No parties, no company. She keeps to herself. Sometimes when she forgets to eat, Mama takes her up a little plate of something. She's not a common drunkard, you understand. She's a lady who's had one sorrow too many. Some people get strong under sorrows. Other people, they snap like twigs, they break, it's not their fault."

"What sorrows?" Meecham said.

"First, they lost their money and then her husband ran away, just left one afternoon while she was at a movie. After that her son went out and got married, left her alone. For nearly a year she was alone and then Earl and his wife came back and they all lived together up in Number Five. That was worse than being alone because there were fights all the time, just words, but loud nasty words, between Earl and his wife, and Earl and his mother, and his mother and his wife. Fighting, fighting, over everything."

"What was his wife's name?"

"Birdie, they called her. Such a silly name. She wasn't anything like a bird. She was a big woman, older than Earl, and quite pleasant unless you crossed her… She had a terrible temper, just terrible. Maybe everything would have worked out, though, if the three of them didn't have to live together, if there wouldn't've been that jealousy between the two women. As it was, Birdie left town—she'd only been here a month or so—and a little while afterwards Earl got a legal notice that she'd divorced him in some other state, Nevada, I think."

"When was that?"

"About two years ago. Upped and left just as suddenly as Mr. Loftus had left. After that Earl began to change. No one knew he was sick, he just got quieter and never went out. First we thought it was sadness over Birdie. He was crazy over her, and when she was in a good mood she babied him and fussed over him like a mother. Mrs. Loftus never babied him, being such a baby herself in some ways. Yes, we thought Earl's trouble was lovesick. But he didn't get any better. One day he went to Arbana, he wanted to look up some books in the University Library, he was always book crazy. He never came back here. He wrote his mother, he paid her rent, everything was friendly, but he never came back. Maybe it was true what Mrs. Loftus told me—that he had to stay there for hospital treatments. But we have a hospital here. So…" He sighed. "Ah well, I'm getting to be an old gossip. More and more, an old gossip." He got up from the davenport and then reached down and patted the cat's head as if apologizing for making too abrupt a move. "I'll go and ask Mama if she saw Mrs. Loftus go out."

When he opened the kitchen door, a rich odor of oil and garlic spilled out, submerging the smell of paint. Meecham went over to the box of kittens and knelt down beside it. They were all asleep now, piled haphazardly on top of one another in a corner. He touched one of them very gently with his forefinger, and immediately the mother cat sauntered over to the box with the casual but alert air of a policeman who doesn't want to start trouble but intends to be around if trouble appears.

Garino returned, followed by a short broad woman in a cotton housedress. She obviously wasn't Italian like her husband. Her hair was light brown, her eyes green, and she had a certain brusqueness of movement and speech that suggested impatience.

Garino started to speak. "Mama said, yes, Mrs. Loftus went out early this morning. To the grocery store, that's what Mama thought, only Mama thought maybe she'd come back again and..."

"I can tell it, Victor," his wife said. "After all, I've got a tongue in my head." She flashed a glance at Meecham. "I guess Victor told you about her?"

"Yes."

"Well, there you have it. When she goes out I never know when she'll come home or how she'll come home or if she'll come home. Nobody knows. She doesn't know herself." Mrs. Garino crossed her arms on her chest with slightly exaggerated belligerence. "She's been gone all day. You know what that means, Victor."

"Yes, Mama."

"Remember last time."

"Yes. Yes, Mama."

"You'd better go and start looking for her."

Garino glanced at Meecham with an air of apology. "Usually she stays in her apartment and drinks quietly by herself. But sometimes..."

"This is a *sometime*," his wife said sharply. "You get your coat on, Victor. You find her. We've got other tenants to consider too. Remember last time."

"What happened last time?" Meecham addressed the question to Garino.

Garino looked down at his hands. "She got in trouble, arrested. After that she was in the hospital for two weeks. She was sick."

"She had the D.T.s." Mrs. Garino's face had gone a little hard. "You hurry up now, Victor."

"All right, all right."

"I'll go with you," Meecham said. "I have to find her anyway."

The woman turned and gave him a long level stare. "Why?"

"I have something for her."

"Money?"

"Yes."

Garino had gone into the next room to get his coat. "She'll blow it all in two days," his wife said in a low voice. "Victor, in there, he thinks I'm getting sour. Yes, and maybe I am. I've got myself to consider too. All this extra work and worry and none of it doing one sliver of good, sure I'm sour. But Victor... Ha, Victor thinks she's a *lady*, and *ladies* don't get to be common ordinary drunks. Ha. Victor's been in this country for twenty years and he still thinks like a Wop, still talks about *ladies*. People are people. Everyone's people."

Garino stood in the doorway with his hat and coat on and a woolen muffler crossed at his neck. "You talk too much, Mama." He added, to Meecham, "Scotch women are jealous."

Mrs. Garino's face was white. "Jealous! Me, jealous!"

"Yes, you are." Garino went over and kissed her affectionately on the forehead. "I'll be back as soon as I can."

"As if I cared."

"You could make some fresh coffee and have it ready."

"I wouldn't make you any coffee for all the money in the world."

"I'm not offering you money."

"Me, jealous. That's funny. That's a scream."

"Get me a clean handkerchief, will you, Mama?"

She went into the next room, muttering under her breath. When she returned with the handkerchief she didn't hand it to

123

him; she threw it at him from the doorway. He caught it, one-handed, and then he went out the door, smiling. Meecham followed him up the steps and through the lobby and into the street.

Garino was still smiling. "Ah, now, you mustn't be embarrassed, Mr. Meecham. That wasn't a quarrel. Mama and I have been married for twenty-one years. When I get home there will be fresh coffee on the stove and I will tell Mama I love her and she will admit she's a little jealous."

"That's all there is to it, eh?"

"Not at first, no. But after twenty-one years we have worked out some short cuts. We have a system."

"My car's across the road," Meecham said.

"We could walk. I know some of the places where she goes, only two or three blocks away. But then, maybe you don't like walking?"

"It's all right for women and children."

They crossed the street and got into Meecham's car.

The old lady and the old memory pierced him like unexpected arrows from a long bow.

"Hey, lady," Charley said. "Wake up. Your bus is leaving."

She moved her head to one side and her hat slipped to the floor, exposing her white silky hair, a little yellowed in places from neglect and curling tongs. Charley bent down to pick up the hat, but he didn't reach it. He straightened up with a grunt of surprise. "Hell, she's drunk. Catch that breath, will you? She's kayoed."

The bus driver, too, had come into the room. He stared down at the woman with his pale lips pressed together in disapproval. "It's a fine thing, isn't it, having people like that hanging around our depot."

"Come on, lady. Wake up now."

"You can just save your breath, Charley. I wouldn't *dream* of taking her on *my* bus, not if she's got thirty tickets."

"Oh, shut up. Give the old girl a break. She's somebody's mother."

"Just so long as she ain't mine," the driver said. "Personally, I've got a good mind to call the police. They know how to deal with people like that."

Charley's face hardened. "Call the police and I'll clobber you. Now get out of here."

"You can't order…"

"Turn blue. Just turn blue."

The driver backed out of the room, still talking, but inaudibly under his breath.

"That stinking lily," Charley said. "I ought to poke him, but I don't want to bust my knuckles."

Meecham was bending over Mrs. Loftus. He had taken off her gloves and was rubbing her small bony hands. The skin felt very dry and cold like a leaf in autumn.

"Mrs. Loftus. Can you hear me?"

She stirred a little, and spoke a name without opening her eyes. "Victor?"

"I'm taking you home, Mrs. Loftus."

She didn't answer.

"Maybe if I opened the window," Charley said, "she'd snap out of it sooner."

"Good idea."

Charley went over and pushed up the window over the washbasin. Fresh snow from the sill sifted into the room like a flight of furry white-winged insects coming to rest. "I never figured she was drunk, see. She's been in a couple of times today and I thought first she was waiting for someone and didn't know what bus to meet. Then, about an hour ago, she comes in the third time, buys a ticket for Arbana and sits down to wait. I kept an eye on her because she looked sick and she acted sick; kept coming in here to the rest room and coming out again. I never for a minute figured she was getting herself hootched."

Meecham picked up the paper bag from the floor and looked inside. It contained a half-empty fifth of cheap rum. He twisted the bag shut again and dropped it into the metal trash container.

"I don't want to hurry you, mister," Charley said. "Nothing like that. Only if she's the mother of a friend of yours like you said, maybe you ought to phone your friend."

"He's out of town. I'll take her home myself."

"I don't want to hurry you, I know you're in a spot. Only there's a little kid out there with her father. You know kids, they're always running to the can. Suppose she comes in here and sees the old lady, it might scare her."

Meecham recalled the gruesome cover of the comic book the little girl had been reading, but he said agreeably, "Yes, it might. I'll do my best."